THE UNDEAD OF NIGHT

Slocum's trigger finger itched with need. He wanted to find Doctor John and send a bullet through his putrid heart. But the voodoo priest was nowhere to be seen. The throne stood empty, its highly polished wood gleaming in the reflected firelight.

An hour of dancing had exhausted the revelers, then the drums suddenly stopped. The worshippers in the clearing dropped to their knees and began a low chant. From the side came Doctor John, flanked by four huge black men stripped to their waists. From the way they walked, Slocum suspected something was wrong with them.

"Behold!" cried Doctor John. "Behold my power!" He drew a knife that gleamed in the moonlight, now giving an eerie illumination to the scene. The voodoo priest raised it, then drove the sharp blade directly into the chest of the man closest to him.

The blade entered the man's chest, then came out bloody—and the man had staggered only slightly.

A zombie! Slocum knew it would be harder stopping Doctor John now that he had four bodyguards of the undead . . .

OTHER BOOKS BY JAKE LOGAN

JAKE LOGAN

RIDE TO VENGEANCE

B

BERKLEY BOOKS, NEW YORK

RIDE TO VENGEANCE

A Berkley Book/published by arrangement with
the author

PRINTING HISTORY
Berkley edition/March 1990

ISBN: 0-425-12010-4

A BERKLEY BOOK® TM 757,375
Berkley Books are published by The Berkley Publishing Group,
200 Madison Avenue, New York, New York 10016.
The name "BERKLEY" and the "B" logo
are trademarks belonging to Berkley Publishing Corporation.

PRINTED IN THE UNITED STATES OF AMERICA

10 9 8 7 6 5 4 3 2 1

RIDE TO VENGEANCE

1

The half-full moon rose, and its silvery light danced across the brown surface of the Mississippi River. John Slocum watched the choppy patterns form and die in muddy eddies. Behind him in the great room of the *Cajun Queen* the passengers danced to the brass band, drank high-priced whiskey, and gambled endlessly. The trip downriver from St. Louis had been profitable for him so far. Tonight would be even better, if he was any judge.

He walked slowly toward the stern of the huge paddle-wheeler. The deck hands below worked tirelessly, feeding the boilers and keeping the giant pistons moving back and forth. He stopped to watch the churning water under the twenty-foot-long blades of the paddlewheel. The silver dropped by the moon vanished in white froth, turned into mist and eerie pale rainbows. The Mississippi River quickly reclamied its due and returned the color to a dark, muddy brown.

"Baton Rouge!" came the cry from the lookout at the prow. The man started calling out depth readings to the daredevil pilot in the cabin on the deck above Slocum. It was foolish to run a riverboat after dark unless you had keen vision and knew the treacheries offered by the river. Slocum wasn't sure about this pilot. The dandy had swaggered aboard upriver from Baton Rouge, as if he owned the ship.

The captain had little to do with the navigation or piloting of the riverboat once they got under way. The pilot was a minor god in the wheelhouse and let everyone know it.

Slocum braced himself against the wrought-iron railing as the *Cajun Queen* began to slow, cutting across the strong current and letting the action of the river push them toward shore.

Lights winked on and off to signal the Baton Rouge dock. The steam whistle blew loudly three times, and the engines cut back. The pilot expertly docked, and the roustabouts began moving heavy crates from the landward side of the riverboat.

Here the captain was in his element. He shouted orders and looked after loading and unloading. He dickered with wood peddlers for the forty-foot lengths of wood stacked along the lower decks needed to run the *Cajun Queen*, then tended to the passengers as they came aboard.

Slocum eyed them critically. Most were riding downriver on the lower decks, not bothering to take fancy staterooms. But there were two men, farmers from their dress, who strutted as they walked. They shouted orders as if they owned the riverboat. A slow smile crept across Slocum's lips. These were men fresh off the farm, with too much money riding in their pockets for their own good. They were reckless and thought they ruled the roost.

He took off his gray Stetson and brushed back lank, black hair, then settled the hat on his head. He had work to do.

Slocum's green eyes cast around the brightly lit dance floor and past the bar to the felt-topped gaming tables. Two were already filled, one with penny-ante poker players and the other with more serious faro players. At a third table, sitting by himself and looking lonesome, was a slender, brown-haired man. He had stacks of chips in front of him which he nervously shuffled. The deck of cards, still in the original wrapper, lay in the middle of the table. The fancy-dressed man didn't seem to notice them.

"Going to do New Orleans up good," one farmer said in a loud voice.

"We deserve it, Josh, we surely do," said the other. "We broke our backs on that dirt farm for too long. Can't imagine our good fortune finding somebody who'd take it off our hands like that."

Slocum saw that the pair were likely brothers. A strong family resemblance carried from their weak chins to their potbellies. They might have been farmers, but they hadn't worked much at it, he reckoned. Slocum had seen too many like the brothers after the war. Their parents had suffered through the hardships, struggling to just stay alive, then their offspring threw away everything the first chance they got.

"Let's get ourselves something to drink, Ben," said the younger of the two. "I'm so thirsty I could drink the *Cajun Queen* dry!"

The pair went to the bar. Slocum snorted in contempt. It didn't take any backbone to belly up to a bar. He waited for them to finish their first round, then sidled up and motioned to the barkeep. "Give my friends a drink on me," he said.

Josh and Ben turned and eyed him suspiciously. Slocum smiled and touched the brim of his hat. "Saw you boys coming aboard at Baton Rouge. You remind me of friends I had once there. Before the war."

"You saw action?" Josh asked.

"Did," Slocum said, not bothering to elaborate. He didn't like to go into what he had done during the war. Riding with Quantrill's Raiders hadn't set well with him, then or now. When he'd protested their bloody-handed ways, they'd gut-shot him and left him for dead. He wasn't proud of it, but he had lived.

"We missed out on killin' them Yanks. They came trompin' through our land, though, and tore up damn near everything," said Ben. "We got lucky and just sold off a sizable chunk."

"Oh?" Slocum's eyebrow arched just enough to keep the man talking. He dropped a gold double eagle on the bar to pay for the drinks.

"We got a relative we're going to see," said Ben.

"We're goin' to New Orleans to get real rich," cut in Josh. "We're gonna be owners of a riverboat, even bigger 'n' better than this one!"

"Do tell. It takes a fair amount of luck to get into that business," Slocum said. "But you boys can do it. I can tell you've got what it takes." Slocum nodded politely to them and went to the table where the gambler sat, still shuffling through the stack of chips. The deck of cards sat forlornly in the center of the green-felt-topped table.

"Looking for a game?" the gambler asked. "I haven't had a spot of luck since I boarded this boat. I'll be damned glad when I reach New Orleans."

"I can do with a little poker," Slocum allowed.

The brothers had followed Slocum over. Josh asked, "Got room for two more?"

"It's a free world," the gambler said. "Leastwise, if you got the money to pay for it." He laughed at his small joke and indicated two chairs for the farmers. They eagerly sat down.

"You said your luck's not running too good," said Ben. "Well, sir, our's is just the reverse of that. We're ridin' a tide that's gonna take us from one end of the Mississippi River to the other."

Slocum opened his coat and settled down for the game. The gambler fanned out his chips and put them in neat piles according to their value. Only then did he seem to notice the deck of cards. "Looks as if the good captain of the *Cajun Queen* has supplied us with these fine paste-boards," he said. "Would you gentlemen care to examine the seal on the pack?"

Ben took the deck and glanced at it. He passed it to Josh, who handed it to Slocum. Slocum knew it hadn't been tampered with. There wasn't any need.

"Let's cut for deal," he said, passing the deck to the gambler. Slocum watched the gambler expertly slice open the deck using his thumbnail. The cards dropped onto the table with a faint hiss. The shuffling went quickly, and Slocum got the deal.

After two hands, Slocum saw how poor the farmers were at draw poker. They had no appreciation of odds and depended on instinct rather than cold logic when they bet. He could have cleaned them out inside an hour if he had been the only one in the game.

The gambler's luck seemed as bad as he had intimated. He lost consistently, just as Slocum won small pots.

The brothers grinned widely as the stack of chips in front of them grew. With their slow increase in wealth came more reckless betting. Slocum took in a deep breath and readied himself for the next hand.

The cards came to him, dealt by Ben. He glanced at them and folded them back, hand resting over them on the table. Slocum opened, then took one card. He glanced at his hand once more. A pair of jacks. He let a small smile creep to the corner of his mouth. As quickly as it appeared, it died.

But Josh had seen it. "You got a good hand, don't you, mister? Well, you're gonna have to work for this pot."

The betting got heavy. Slocum finally folded after see-ing most of the farmer's money go into the pot. That left Josh and the gambler.

"Thought you were holding too much to back out. No nerve," said Josh.

"I got more than nerve," the gambler said. "I got the winning hand."

"No way! I got a full house!" Josh dropped his cards to the table and started to scoop up his winnings.

"Doesn't beat four treys," said the gambler, showing his hand.

"He was the one who had the good hand," protested Josh, pointing at Slocum.

"I didn't," said Slocum. "I've folded and don't have to show you what I had, but . . ." He turned over his discarded hand and showed the pair of jacks. "I was just bluffing."

"You had a good hand. I knew I could beat you!"

"You did. That's my money in the pot, too," Slocum said. "He won fair and square. Four of a kind is a mighty strong hand, no matter what your hand is."

Ben and Josh looked at the pile of money they'd lost. Josh jumped to his feet. "You can't take that! It's ours! That's all we got for sellin' the family farm!"

"You bet, you lost," the gambler said, pulling the money off the table.

"You cheated us!" cried Ben.

Slocum was on his feet and had his Colt Navy in his hand before either of the farmers could drag out the pistols they had stuck in their belts.

"There wasn't any cheating in this game," he said. "You lost, same as I did. If you didn't want to lose, you shouldn't have played."

"He cheated us! You, too!"

The captain and several of the crew came over to see what the commotion was about.

"Captain, this tinhorn swindled us!"

"That so?" the captain asked, staring at Slocum's drawn six-shooter.

"No, it isn't. Those two—and I—lost fair and square. Can't say I like it, but I knew the odds. They don't seem to."

"We don't cotton to sore losers aboard the *Cajun Queen*," the captain said gruffly. "If you gentleman will step over to the bar, I'll buy you a drink. If not, let's go outside and cool off."

Slocum saw that this wasn't a polite invitation. The riverboat's captain was telling the farmers to either quiet down and get drunk sociably or he'd throw them off the boat. The brothers grumbled and went to the bar.

"Many thanks," the gambler said. "That was getting out of hand."

Slocum said nothing. He returned his pistol to its soft leather cross-draw holster. From across the room the two farmers glared at him. Slocum didn't much care. He settled down at a table and let a waitress bring him a neat bourbon. He knocked back the whiskey and ordered another. Before it came, he saw that the farmers and the gambler were gone.

Cursing, he dropped a few coins on the table and rushed from the room. It took his eyes several seconds to adjust to the darkness outside. When they did he hurried toward the stern of the riverboat, where three figures huddled.

"Our money, you damned thief!" demanded Ben, holding his six-shooter to the gambler's head.

"You cheated us. We want our money back—and everything else you got on you!" demanded Josh.

"So you're not just lousy gamblers and poor losers but are also thieves," the gambler said equably.

"Let's throw him into the river," said Ben. "Nobody'd ever miss his worthless carcass."

Even above the loud thrashing of the paddlewheel, the cocking of Slocum's six-shooter rang out, deadly and menacing.

"You gents better leave him alone or there's going to be two bodies in the Mississippi River. And they're not likely to be doing much swimming for shore with a couple of lead slugs in them," he said.

Ben turned and looked square down the barrel of Slocum's pistol. His own six-shooter started around but the gambler knocked it aside.

"Throw it overboard," Slocum said. "The pistol, not its owner, though I don't now why I'm drawing the line there."

"You can't!" wailed Ben. "That was my pa's gun!"

The gun vanished into the river without a trace. Josh's followed with less complaint than from his brother. Slocum decided this wasn't a family heirloom.

"You two run along, like the captain told you," said Slocum. "You give this man—or me—any more trouble and it'll be the last thing you ever do." The way John Slocum spoke told the two farmers this was no idle threat. That they escaped with their lives now was nothing short of a miracle and a reflection on their true good luck.

"Thanks, John," the gambler said when the brothers had vanished back into the *Cajun Queen*'s ballroom. "I thought they'd stayed inside to get drunk. I didn't hear them coming after me."

"It's all right, Preston. We've been looking out for each other since St. Louis, and it's worked out just fine."

"You want to divvy the take now?" Preston Chambers asked his friend.

"Later, when we dock in New Orleans."

"This is the sweetest trip down the river I've ever taken," said Chambers. "You set those two up so slick it made my heart want to leap out of my chest. They thought it was you they had to beat. They didn't pay me no never mind till I dropped those four treys on the table."

"You hadn't been winning," said Slocum, "and I had. They thought I was their only competition." He snorted in disgust. The farmers had no idea of the odds against them in the game. It wouldn't have mattered if Slocum had won or lost. He and Preston Chambers were partners and would split the take, whoever won. It had just happened that he had been able to set Chambers up for the kill tonight. It had worked the other way round on other nights during the trip.

"I don't think we'll be troubled by those hayseeds again," Chambers said, lighting a cheroot. He puffed contentedly for a minute, then said, "I'm going to my state-room. I want to be fresh for New Orleans when we dock tomorrow." Preston Chambers looked around, then flicked the ash into the froth created by the paddlewheel. "You might as well turn in, too, John. Those two won't give us any more trouble."

Slocum wasn't so sure.

2

The *Cajun Queen* hove into view of the port at the Julia Street docks just after sunrise. Slocum had been unable to sleep for more than a few minutes at a stretch in the overly soft bed in his cabin. Even though he was surrounded by the finest things he could imagine, he continued to worry. He and Preston Chambers had worked a good racket all the way down the Mississippi River. Although both men were fully capable of cheating at cards if they had to, neither had on this trip. Simply working as a team and splitting their take had been enough.

Slocum thought the riverboat's captain had caught on to their scheme. The grizzled old veteran of the river had seen and done well nigh everything in his day. Slocum had heard the captain talking to several passengers about running Yankee blockades during the war and getting through to the beleaguered Confederate forces at Biloxi. If he had done that, a few cardsharps out to bamboozle the unwary wouldn't trouble him any.

Slocum rolled out of the featherbed and found his polished boots just inside the door. He dressed quickly. He had much to do today. Slocum settled his cross-draw holster and made sure the ebony-handled Colt rested easy. In spite of all that Chambers had said, Slocum expected more trouble from the two farmers. It wouldn't hurt either him or Chambers to get off the *Cajun Queen* before the sodbusters could raise any kind of fuss about double-dealing gamblers.

Throwing his belongings into the bag he carried, Slocum made his way out into the riverboat's great room. The barkeep stood polishing glasses. Other than the solitary man, there were only memories of the gaiety that had gone on here the night before. Slocum went and rapped sharply on Chambers' door. The sooner they left the riverboat, the sooner they could divide the take. Slocum had no qualms about Chambers keeping their stake; he had known the man for years and knew he was honest.

Slocum smiled crookedly. Preston Chambers was as honest as any riverboat gambler ever could be.

"You there, Preston?" he called when the man didn't answer the knock. Slocum put down his bag and drew his pistol. He didn't like the silence from within.

He rapped again. This time there came a furtive scurrying sound. He tried the door and found it locked. With a hard kick, Slocum knocked the door inward on its hinges. The door smashed against the wall and broke a full-length mirror. Cascades of glass came down, but Slocum avoided them, his six-shooter level and ready for action.

A shrill, indignant shriek filled the room. "Preston, whatevah *is* this man doing heah?"

The red-haired woman in Preston Chambers' bed pulled the bedclothes up to her chin. Slocum saw that she was naked and more angry than frightened at his intrusion.

From the vanity adjoining the sleeping room came Chambers, the barrel of a large-caliber pistol preceding him. When he saw Slocum standing in the doorway, the six-shooter vanished.

"You'll be the death of me yet, John," the gambler said. "My friend stayed a bit longer than I'd thought. . . ." He let his sentence trail off as he smiled broadly. "I'm sure you wouldn't mind if we took a few more minutes to get ready for . . . docking."

"Sorry," Slocum said. "Didn't mean to intrude. I'm anxious to get off the boat." He gave the redhead a long, lingering look. The woman's hot stare back contained no more anger. She looked to be on the verge of asking him to stay.

Slocum ducked out of the room before she could speak. He didn't remember seeing her on the riverboat, but Chambers had found her—and Slocum didn't butt in on another man's woman. Even if that woman was just for the night.

He sighed and looked around. The barkeep had continued shining his glasses, unperturbed over all that had happened. Slocum pulled the door to Chamber's stateroom shut the best he could. He hoped neither of them inside cut their feet on the broken glass.

Slocum picked up his bag and went to the outer deck. Leaning over the rail he saw the docks in the misty distance. It'd be a good hour or more before the *Cajun Queen* came to port. He wanted nothing more than dry land under his boots again. He had been on the Mississippi River too long for his taste.

The deck hands worked to get the steam capstan in order. Others began milling around below, muttering among themselves. Slocum took a deep whiff and knew the reason for the gathering. The savory smell of cooking food from the galley one deck lower made his mouth water. If he had to wait for Chambers to finish with his woman, the time might as well be spent constructively.

Finding a vacant table in the elegant dining room proved easy this early in the morning. The simple fare prepared on this last day before docking suited Slocum just fine. The rasher of bacon, the two fried eggs, and the fried potatoes filled him better than the riverboat's usually fancy menu.

He finished off a second cup of strong black coffee and felt better than he had in days. Land was in sight, and he had a full belly. Chambers had more than five hundred dollars of his money, and all New Orleans waited for him.

Slocum wasn't sure what he'd do once he got to the Crescent City. Gamble a mite to add to his stake, he knew. Then he thought he might drift westward into Texas before the Louisiana summer heat and humidity got too oppressive.

He'd earned his money these past few weeks and intended to spend it wisely. A slow smile crossed his lips. The woman in Chambers' bed had been pretty enough. She might want to help him get rid of some of the money, if she didn't intend to stay with the gambler when they left the riverboat.

Heaving to his feet, Slocum grabbed his bag and went back onto the second deck. He ran into the red-haired woman and almost knocked her down.

"Sorry," he said, helping her regain her balance. She had dressed. From the cut of her simple frock, he knew she worked the river and wasn't a bored passenger wanting to spend the time with an exciting gambler like Preston Chambers.

"You seem to be intent on bulling your way in on me, sir," she said. The words were harsh, but the smile on her face softened any insult. "Why don't you make amends by buying me breakfast?"

Slocum glanced over the woman's shoulder toward the New Orleans dock area. The *Cajun Queen* was still more than a half hour from docking. He held out his arm, and the woman accepted it graciously.

They chatted idly while she hungrily devoured a breakfast even larger than the one Slocum had just finished. He sipped at a third cup of coffee.

"So there's no way you'd like to take a few days to properly show me the city?" he asked as she was finishing, having gotten no farther than the woman's name.

"Sir, I would enjoy that more than anything else," she said, "but I cannot. Captain Stephan is adamant about the terms of my, uh, employment. I owe him much."

"From the war?" Slocum asked.

The expressionless mask that fell told him more than simple words. Whatever the captain had done, this woman felt she owed him everything. She would even be his ship's whore.

"I must speak with the captain. Thank you for your charity, sir."

"It's been my pleasure." Slocum watched the redhead bustle off in search of the *Cajun Queen*'s officer. He mentally amended his statement. He had bought her breakfast. The real pleasure had belonged solely to Preston Chambers.

Slocum started out once more to find his partner. The riverboat's whistle sounded loudly, and then the boat lurched as the pilot brought the *Cajun Queen* into dock. The sharp jolt caused Slocum to grab for a rail. He rode out the moment of getting the large paddlewheeler secured, then started around to return to Chambers' stateroom. There wasn't any reason they couldn't leave now.

Slocum had food in his belly and had satisfied himself about the red-haired woman's inability to accompany him into New Orleans. And Chambers had no doubt just satisfied himself.

It was high time they moved on.

Loud voices carried, even over the din of the steam capstan working to unload the heavy bales at the prow of the riverboat. Slocum stopped and peered over the railing. The two farmers shouted and gestured wildly at a tall, burly man who had been the first up the gangplank. The three men vanished under the walkway.

"Sir, a word with you."

Slocum turned and looked over his shoulder. Captain Stephan and his first officer came up.

"What can I do for you, Captain?" Slocum asked. He wondered if this had anything to do with having breakfast with the redhead. The captain couldn't be the jealous type, not knowing what the woman did aboard his vessel.

"I wanted to be sure you were leaving the *Cajun Queen*, Mr. Slocum," the officer said. "We try to please." The captain cleared his throat and looked around.

Slocum had no idea what Captain Stephan wanted.

"There is the matter of a small gratuity for allowing you and Mr. Chambers to operate aboard my ship," the officer said more bluntly.

"Had you and Chambers come to this agreement back in St. Louis?" Slocum asked, beginning to understand. The captain expected a bribe for not interfering with them as they worked the passengers who wanted excitement rather than winnings.

"He had, sir. Now that we have docked and I have other matters to attend to, I wish you to take care of it. Immediately."

"Mr. Chambers has my share. I'll have to get it from him."

"Do hurry, Mr. Slocum. "We'll be waiting for you at the gangway."

As Slocum brushed past, the junior officer beside the captain took his bag. Slocum started to protest, then bit back his anger. That bag contained all he owned in the world. He saw it would be in good hands until he talked with Preston Chambers and found out what amount of money the captain had deemed fair for allowing them to ply their trade on the cruise from St. Louis.

Slocum went into the great room and paused. The two farmers and their burly companion stood at the far end of the room. Their voices echoed the length of it—and he didn't like the sound of what he heard. His hand drifted down and unfastened the leather thong over the hammer of his six-shooter.

Slocum hadn't got halfway across the dance floor when

they spotted him. Josh turned to his brother and tugged on his sleeve. Ben turned, frightened, and ran like a scalded dog. Josh wasn't far behind. Their powerfully built, dark-haired companion paused, then took off after them. Slocum thought the man looked as if he was itching for a fight.

And from the way he was built, he could have given Slocum a hard time. Why hadn't he?

Slocum went to Chambers' stateroom and started to knock. The door hung askew from where he had kicked it in earlier—and there was something else.

In a swift movement, Slocum had his pistol out and ready. He again used his foot to open the door. This time there wasn't a sultry redhead inside. Preston Chambers lay sprawled face-down across the bed, his throat cut. The blood had gushed out and soaked into the soft feather mattress.

Slocum slipped into the room and pushed the door shut behind him. It took him only a few seconds to realize that Chambers had been robbed. The man's wallet was gone—and so was Slocum's share of their winnings.

Slocum holstered his six-shooter and rolled his friend over. He took an involuntary step back at what he found. He had seen men in worse condition than this during the war.

John Slocum had never seen a man with his throat slit and a dried chicken claw stuffed into his mouth.

3

Slocum stared at the chicken claw in Preston Chambers' mouth and shuddered. This was no way for a man to die. That his throat had been slit was bad enough. To defile the body with the claw turned Slocum's stomach.

He spun and rushed to the door. The only people aboard the *Cajun Queen* likely to want Chambers dead were the two farmers and their vicious-looking friend who had just boarded the riverboat. Slocum ran to the far end of the great room and burst through the glass doors. They rattled but didn't break as they slammed against the walls.

Six-shooter clutched firmly in his hand, Slocum went stalking the trio. At the front of the walkway he leaned over the fancy iron railing and peered down to the lower deck. Ben, Josh, and the mysterious third man stood below talking—arguing again, if Slocum was any judge.

Ben looked up and saw Slocum hanging on the railing like an avenging angel. He yelled, and the three men ducked into the forest of crates and bales stored on the cargo deck. Slocum cursed his bad luck but wasn't going to lose them—not if they had so brutally murdered his friend.

Vaulting the railing, Slocum landed hard on the lower deck. The shock jolted him enough to make him lose his balance. Because of this, luck rode with him. A knife whistled through the air and stuck in the cotton bale to his right. If he had kept his balance, he would have sprouted the steel blade from his chest.

Slocum cocked his Colt but found no target. Not wanting to waste bullets by firing blindly, he didn't squeeze off a random shot to flush his quarry. All around him roustabouts worked to move the *Cajun Queen*'s cargo to the Julia Street docks. Slocum didn't want to kill a crewman when he wanted the thieving, murdering farmers and their friend.

Shoulders brushing the close-packed crates, Slocum started on his quest. Hunting the three down wouldn't be too hard, he figured. All it would take was a spot of caution and some more luck.

Ben flashed across his field of vision, darting from one stack of crates to another. Slocum got off a shot but missed. He ran parallel to the fleeing farmer, then worked his way forward on the deck.

A shadow warned him he had fallen into a trap. Slocum doubled up, rolled, and began firing his six-shooter until it was empty. A baling hook slashed across his back but didn't do more than catch the fabric of his jacket. He was rewarded with a grunt and knew he had wounded his attacker.

Slocum came to his feet, his pistol empty. Josh hunched over, clutching his belly.

"You gut-shot my brother, you son of a bitch!" roared Ben. The farmer came at him with a gleaming knife.

Slocum would have shot his legs out from under him, then put a bullet through his head—if his pistol had been loaded. Instead he caught and turned the reckless charge, using an upthrust right arm to block the descending knife and slide it away from his body. He drove his left fist into Ben's midriff as hard as he could. The blubber he had suspected there absorbed the force of his blow, but it did send the wild-eyed farmer reeling.

Grabbing the man's wrist, Slocum wrestled the knife from his hand. It fell to the deck with a loud clatter.

"Why did you kill Chambers like that?" he demanded. "He was my friend. You're going to pay."

Ben lay on his back, gasping for breath. Josh moaned loudly, still clutching his stomach where Slocum's slug had caught him.

Slocum stuffed his Colt Navy back into its holster and picked up the fallen knife. He advanced on Ben, intent on gutting the man if he didn't talk—and maybe even if he did.

"What in hell's goin' on back here?" demanded a loud voice.

The deck officer had heard the shots and had come to investigate. Slocum hurried to Ben's side and put the knife to the farmer's throat. "How's it feel?" he asked. "Did you give Chambers time to think about it before you slit his throat?"

A heavy boot crunched into Slocum's side, sending him spinning. The knife slipped from his hand and clattered overboard. He rolled and came to his feet, ready for a fight. The man he had seen with the two farmers towered over him.

The meaty fist was already on its way when Slocum regained his balance. It crashed into the side of his head and decked him again. Dazed and eyes fogged with pain, Slocum tried to shake off the effects of the blow and get back into the fight. He couldn't let Chambers' killers escape.

"I said, what's going on here?"

Slocum lashed out blindly, his fists hitting a glancing blow. Then he thought he was going to die. Boots came at him from all sides. A fist drove him back to the deck. Then two more struck him in the chest and side. He rolled into a tight ball, then exploded, arms and legs driving out forcefully.

This drove back his attackers long enough for him to grab a cotton bale and pull himself upright. Slocum turned and faced the men arrayed around him in a half circle. To his surprise, they were all roustabouts, members of the *Cajun Queen*'s crew.

"Hold on!" boomed a familiar voice. "Don't gut the son of a bitch yet." Captain Stephan strode into view. "I might have known it'd be you. You and that good-for-nothing tinhorn friend of yours had to be pure trouble."

"The farmers," Slocum gasped out. "The two hayseeds and their friend. They killed Chambers."

"What are you blathering about?" the captain demanded.

"I tried to stop them from leaving the ship. I don't know what they're up to, but they killed Chambers and—"

"What's this about the gambler man being dead?" Captain Stephan's cold eyes bored into Slocum's equally cold green ones.

"In his cabin. They slit his throat. I tried to stop them from escaping. Shot one and was about to take care of the other when their friend jumped me."

"Did you see anyone else?" Stephan demanded of his deck officer. The weathered, gaunt man shook his head.

"They were here. They can't have gone far," Slocum insisted. He started to go after them himself, but one of the crew shoved him back against the bale.

"Go look for them. You know the pair. The dirt farmers we picked up in Baton Rouge." Stephan sent his deck officer scuttling away to find Ben and Josh. The roustabouts didn't move. They still held Slocum a prisoner in the center of the tight circle.

"I winged the one," Slocum repeated, still trying to get his wits about him. His chest burned, and he had bruises forming where he had received the many kicks and blows.

"We might have to hold you for the authorities," Captain Stephan said.

"They're the ones who killed Chambers!"

"About that," Stephan said, "let's go look. Where did you say the so-called murder take place?"

"In his stateroom. And there's nothing 'so-called' about it." Slocum gritted his teeth and let two of the deck hands help him through the maze of crates. Captain Stephan walked briskly up the wrought-iron steps to the upper deck. He stopped when his officer came running up, out of breath.

"We searched the *Queen* from stem to stern, Cap'n," the mate reported. "We didn't find the farmers anywhere. The cargo officer said he thought they'd left right after we docked."

"They were—" Slocum wasn't allowed to finish. The river man holding his right arm tightened his grip painfully.

"Very well. It's for the best, I think, that they are gone." Stephan shot a disgusted look in Slocum's direction. "Let's speak with your gambler friend. Perhaps he can shed more light on this matter."

"He's dead, damn it!"

Slocum, three of the crew, and the first officer followed Stephan through the great room to Chambers' stateroom. The captain pushed open the damaged door and saw Chambers' body lying on the bed in the pool of dried blood.

"Damnation!" the captain cursed. "This place is a mess. It'll cost a fortune refitting it."

"A man has been killed," Slocum said angrily. "Doesn't that mean anything to you?"

"It means trouble with the New Orleans police." Captain Stephan went over to Chambers. The grotesque chicken claw still protruded from the dead man's mouth.

The three crewmen backed out of the cabin. Two of the river men crossed themselves as they left. The third, a black man, fell to his knees and banged his head on the floor, chanting something Slocum couldn't understand.

"*Gris-gris*," Stephan muttered.

"What?"

"Bad *gris-gris*," he repeated. "I knew you two were trouble when you boarded in St. Louis."

"What's *gris-gris* mean?" Slocum asked.

"Close this cabin immediately," Stephan ordered his mate. "No one comes in. See to cleaning this *mess* up personally. Don't go shooting off your fat mouth about it, either, or I'll cut your tongue out." He glared at the three roustabouts. The captain didn't have to threaten them. They were at the point of turning tail and running. The two still muttered heartfelt prayers and the black roustabout stood staring at the chicken claw.

"You're not going to let them get away with this, are you?" Slocum stared at Stephan, horrified at what he'd just heard. The *Cajun Queen*'s captain wasn't going to inform the New Orleans authorities about Chambers' brutal death. He was going to hide it and let the brothers get away scot-free!

"Get away with what?" Stephan asked. He was still pale. He turned and looked back at Chambers. "This is very bad *gris-gris*. None of our business. And, sir, I'd advise you not to meddle."

"But—"

"This had nothing to do with the two farmers," Stephan said positively. "They wouldn't do this."

"Then it was the man with them."

Captain Stephan motioned impatiently and the two nearest roustabouts grabbed Slocum's arms and carried him out of the stateroom and out to the walkway.

"You're not getting rid of me this easily," Slocum declared.

"Pay your ticket," the captain said coldly.

"It was paid in St. Louis!"

"It was not paid," Stephan said. "Your friend was going to pay both my, uh, gratuity and your fares when we arrived in New Orleans. Considering his condition, I won't ask for his passage fare. But you have to pay."

"He had all our money, and he was robbed!"

"He ain't gonna pay, Cap'n," said the mate. "Should we . . . collect?"

"No, we have his baggage. Sir, when you pay the thirty dollars for the passage from St. Louis, I will return your property. Until then, leave the *Cajun Queen*."

"I don't have any money. And everything I own is in that bag."

"We expect to leave port in one week's time. Your property becomes mine at that time, unless you have paid in full. I think this is extremely generous on my part considering all that has happened."

"Captain!" Slocum's pleas fell on deaf ears. The roustabouts grabbed him again and gave him the bum's rush down the gangplank and to the dock. They shoved hard enough to send him sprawling face-down in a puddle of sewage.

Slocum got to his feet and brushed himself off the best he could. He seethed at the indignity and injustice of all that had happened to him—and Preston Chambers—that day. And John Slocum wasn't a man to take any of this lightly.

4

It occurred to Slocum that he couldn't even reload his Colt Navy. All his spare ammunition was in the bag Captain Stephan had impounded aboard the *Cajun Queen*. He reached behind and under his coat and touched the thick-bladed knife sheathed at the small of his back. This would have to keep him alive in New Orleans until he got the money to buy a few rounds.

Rummaging through his pockets, he checked his other resources. Less than four dollars was all the stake he had. He hadn't spent lavishly the night before aboard the river-boat, but he had "lost" a fair amount to Chambers in the card game. Slocum was sorry now that he hadn't taken his friend up on the offer to divide their take rather than waiting until they reached the Delta city.

His once fine livery was dirty and torn. That didn't bother him as much as the lack of ammunition. He wasn't likely to be hanging around high society, but he did wish he had taken a bath. He reeked from wallowing in the filth on the deck and dock of the riverboat.

Straightening his clothing as much as he could, Slocum went off to find the farmers and their murderous friend. The few inquiries he made along the docks got him nowhere. By midday his belly was starting to complain, but he was loathe to spend the little money he had. He'd need that as seed money.

Slocum stopped a passing dock worker and asked, "Pardon me. Where do I ask around here for work?"

The black man looked at him as if he were a three-headed pig, then laughed. "What foah the likes of you want a job down heah? This heah dock's for us black folk. Not you." Showing strong white teeth and laughing uproariously, the man went back to his work.

Slocum had to admit that the dock man was right. He hadn't seen any whites loading or unloading cargo from the paddlewheelers in port along the Julia Street docks. And the pay was likely to be too low to do him any good. Even at a munificent fifty cents a day of backbreaking labor, he couldn't get enough money fast enough to rescue his bag from the *Cajun Queen*.

He needed thirty dollars in less than a week or Captain Stephan was likely to take anything of value in the bag and toss the rest overboard into the Mississippi River.

Slocum seethed with the injustice of all that had happened to him. Chambers had died—and now Slocum found himself destitute. In that large bag were his spare Colt Navy, clothing, and what few mementos he had of his parents, dead since the war. His hand dropped to his waistcoat pocket and touched the lump there. At least he still had his brother Robert's watch. This was all that remained of his family, except for the lingering memories.

Hanging around the docks wasn't going to solve any of his problems. If he wanted work, he'd have to find it elsewhere. He had planned to come to New Orleans and pass some time in the dives of the Vieux Carré, gambling, whoring, and spending the money he had made on the trip down the Mississippi. All that was behind him. He had to make new plans, plans for getting the money he needed.

Even though four dollars wasn't likely to buy him much in a city as expensive as New Orleans, he knew he had to make a start somewhere. Slocum walked up Julia Street, crossed to Canal, then cut down Royal and entered a different world.

The docks had been bustling with life, thriving with the pulse of a dynamic city rebuilding after the war. As he walked along the Rue Royal and looked up at the buildings' ornate wrought-iron railings, red-tiled roofs, and French- and Spanish-style houses and businesses, he wondered where everyone had gone. He might have entered a ghost town.

Near the Place d'Armes he slowed and looked across the plaza toward the Cathedral of St. Louis. A funeral was in progress. Slocum frowned. Or was it a wedding? A brass band waited outside the church in the shade. When the pallbearers carried out the coffin, the band struck up a funeral dirge. The cortege started up St. Anne, going toward a cemetery. As they turned the corner, the dirge changed to a more lively jazz tune. Slocum watched in fascination. A band at a funeral?

The funeral might explain the lack of people in the streets, but he doubted it. The heat was already oppressive, and the humidity caused sweat to remain on his face and stain his clothing.

Slocum struck out and went deeper into the French Quarter. He had heard of Gallatin Street and its reputation. The dives were mostly closed, but a few people stirred here and there.

"Pardon me," he said, stopping a man in the street. "Why is everything shut up today?"

The man looked around, as if it hadn't occurred to him. Then he gave Slocum the once-over and said, "You got to be new here. Nothing's happenin' in the Vieux Carré till nightfall. Then the place comes alive. Let me give you a bit of advice."

"What?" Slocum asked, cautious of any advice.

"You won't last a second along Gallatin Street. Go find yourself a nice place to stay. Why, some of the dives here sell wine for two dollars a glass!"

"I could use something cheaper," Slocum allowed.

"Here, come along. Let me show you a nice place, a place for a gentleman like you."

The man motioned for Slocum to follow. They walked down Gallatin Street to an alley. "Down here," the man said. "A nice place, a good, cheap place to wet your whistle. Not the best whiskey, but it's only a nickel a shot."

Down the alley Slocum saw a variety of places clustered in a one-block area. The Blue Light, the Amsterdam, Archie Murphy's, the Stockhold, the Baltimore—all places he'd need a loaded six-shooter before entering.

He turned in time to see the man slipping a slung shot from his inner pocket. Slocum reacted instinctively, drawing his pistol and cocking it. The man blanched as he returned the blackjack to his pocket.

"No need to get all flighty on me now," he said. "I was just checking my own armaments."

Slocum realized how close he had come to getting robbed. If the would-be thief had realized the pistol wasn't loaded, Slocum would have been out everything he had remaining—including his life.

Slocum positioned himself at the corner of Girod Street and watched the French Quarter slowly come alive. The farther the ruddy sun dipped down toward the horizon, the more people came out from their quiet, cool residences. By the time the sun had vanished and the heat had waned, bright gaslights popped on all over the Vieux Carré. Hundreds thronged the narrow cobblestone streets and began a night of revelry such as Slocum had expected to be enjoying.

Whores walked the street, their "fancy men" watching closely who they approached. If the women left with a river man, they were back on the street in a few minutes.

Slocum didn't doubt that more than one sailor and river man had fallen victim to a woman's wiles and her pimp's cudgel along these streets.

Of the saloons he watched, Slocum decided the one best for his limited bankroll was the Green Tree Dance Hall on Girod. The customers going and coming didn't look too prosperous, but they had some money to spend. And the man outside hawking attractions inside hinted at big money to be won gambling.

Slocum entered the dimly lit saloon and found what the main attraction was. In the back of the saloon was a deep pit. The bar's patrons surrounded it, yelling and placing bets on what went on below them. Slocum pushed through the crowd and saw a savage dog ripping apart wharf rats.

"Bet, mister? That's not just any dog down there. That's O'Neil's dog, Twitcher, and he's going for the record. Bet you five dollars he don't make it."

"What's the record?" Slocum asked, staring at the bloody remains of more than three dozen rats in the pit. The dog's ferocity knew no bounds. It barely finished breaking the back of one rat when it moved on to another.

"Sixty rats in five minutes. Twitcher's been at it almost four minutes now. He ain't gonna make it!"

"I'll see that if you give me three-to-one odds!" cried another patron.

Slocum hung back, unsure of the bet. He preferred cards, where he knew the odds. The cry went up less than a minute later. Twitcher had failed to kill five dozen rats in five minutes—but he had missed the mark by only two rodents.

"You shoulda seen the brawl when Twitcher went up against Hanley's dog, Cabbage, over in the Amsterdam Dance Hall," the man said. "That was a battle royal."

"I'm sure it was," Slocum said. The stench of blood and death from the pit made his nose twitch. He'd seen bloodier sports in his day, but it was apparent they were going to keep the dog in the pen it until it dropped from exhaustion.

"You look like a man willing to place a bet or two," the man said. "But this ain't your cup of tea, is it?"

"Not really. Can't rightly size up the contestants," Slocum said.

"Come on over here." The man put his arm around Slocum's shoulders. Slocum shrugged once and got free. He didn't want the man close to him, especially when he felt light fingers working toward his pocket watch.

"No need to get riled, mister," the man said, edging away when he saw Slocum's expression. This wasn't the kind of place to let anyone get close.

The sudden dull report of gunshots echoing through the saloon brought Slocum wheeling about. The crowd cheered and carried on and didn't seem disturbed about the gunfire. Slocum went to the other side of the saloon and looked down into another pit. More dead rats, but this time it was the spectators doing the killing.

"Want to try your luck, mister?" asked the man running the bizarre game. He held out a small-bore rifle. "Fifty cents ante. You get that back after ten rats, then it's a dollar for every ten additional ones you shoot."

"Your bullets?" Slocum asked.

"My bullets, my game."

Slocum looked around and saw dozens of men placing bets as on the final number of rats to be hit. The man before him hadn't reached ten; the huge black wharf rats were energetic and hard to stop with the small-caliber slugs.

"I'll give it a try," Slocum said.

"Side bet?"

"A dollar that I make it to fifteen," Slocum said, putting his money on a battered, beer-stained table. He hefted the rifle, saw that the front sights were slightly askew, and knew he had to ignore them. After checking the loads and the line of the barrel to be sure it wouldn't blow up in his hands, he set to work.

During the war he had been a sniper—and one of the

best. Waiting for Yankee officers and their gold braid to glint in the sun before shooting wasn't any more challenging than shooting the chittering, snarling rats in the pit.

"You made fifteen," the man running the game called. "Five dollars says you can't make another fifteen."

Slocum saw that the betting increased when he hit twenty. At thirty the crowd was going wild. He had no idea what the record was, but he must be nearing it. He reloaded several times, often discarding defective cartridges.

"Want to try for fifty, mister? I say you can't do it!"

The bets flowed like the Mississippi River. Deeper, thicker, the greenbacks poured onto the table. By the time Slocum had won twenty dollars, he had blasted sixty-two rats.

"You can't quit now," protested the barker. "I'm making a fortune off you! You can't miss."

Slocum took his money and folded the scrip, stashing it in his shirt pocket. "This'll do me just fine for the moment," he said. "I might mosey back later on after I've wet my whistle."

"Do that," the man said earnestly. In the same breath, he called out, "Who can beat the champ? Sixty-two rats! Who can beat him? You, son, you do it?" The barker fixed his attention on a wet-behind-the ears youth fresh off a sailing ship.

Slocum drifted away, not intending to buy any liquor. He was disgusted with the slaughter, even of the vicious rats. Still, it had put precious money in his pocket. He could find a card game and double his money and have enough to ransom his bag from Captain Stephan.

First he wanted to find a general store and get loads for his Colt Navy. He felt naked walking around Gallatin Street without a working six-shooter.

Slocum stepped out into the sultry New Orleans night and sucked in the heavy air. The smell of sewage running in the streets didn't please him. He preferred the cleanness of the range, the high snowcapped mountains, even the dry

desert to city life. There were advantages to this town,
though.

He returned the smile of a passing painted woman.
Looking around, Slocum found the whore's pimp watching
intently from across the street. He tipped his hat to the
woman and kept walking. He needed ammunition more
than he needed recreation at the moment.

He turned away from Gallatin Street and turned down
Girod, going past Mother Colby's Sure Enuf Hotel and the
smaller, less pretentious House of Rest for Weary Boatmen
across the street. Both were three stories tall and looked
like the kind of place where you went in healthy and came
out dead. Saloons and brothels abounded, but he couldn't
find a store selling ammunition.

"Hey, mister, come on in," yelled a man in front of a
saloon on the corner of Gallatin Street and Barracks. "A
nickel buys you all you can drink. You look like you could
break the house. Try us!"

Slocum walked past. The first drink might be laced with
knockout drops. The saloon had that look.

"What are you, a temperance woman? A pussy? You got
any balls dangling between your legs?" The man's insults
stopped when he found another likely customer for the
dive. Slocum shook his head. Where did all the victims
come from? It hardly seemed there were that many ships in
the port or that many gullible dupes in New Orleans.

He stopped and frowned when he glanced back down
the two blocks that comprised Gallatin Street. He could see
from Barracks all the way to Hospital. A bobbing head in
the crowd had caught his eye.

Slocum turned back down Gallatin. Dark alleys led in
either direction from the bustling, packed street. The dark-
haired man he had spotted had turned down one of them.
Slocum glanced at the signpost and saw he was on Levee
Street. That meant nothing to him. That he wended his way
through the crowd and ended up in front of Bill Swan's
Fireproof Coffee House meant nothing either.

That he followed the man he had seen on the *Cajun Queen* with the two farmers did.

Slocum touched the butt of his Colt Navy and remembered he didn't have any shells for it. That mattered less to him at the moment than finding the burly man who had entered the saloon.

He went inside.

5

Bill Swan's Fireproof Coffee House didn't seem any different from the other dives along Gallatin Street. The boisterous crowd of sailors enjoying themselves as they got drunker and drunker seemed to be everywhere. Slocum looked around the large room for his quarry. Crimes against persons went unnoticed. The six bouncers constantly roving the room stopped any damage to the property. Other than these brawny six men carrying ax handles as weapons, used frequently and vigorously, the law was absent.

This suited Slocum just fine. He didn't want to explain to an officious policeman why he wanted to beat the hell out of the man he had followed inside.

Slocum edged along the walls, eyes raking the crowd for sign of the man from the *Cajun Queen*. He didn't see his quarry. Sitting down at one of the few empty tables in the saloon, he put his back to a wall and watched the ebb and flow of the crowd. Most of the customers were sailors. A few looked to be river men fresh off the Mississippi.

37

Only a few had the aspect of locals about them—and all these were preying on the others.

"It's always been like this," said a man standing to one side and watching the crowd, too. "We're like vultures. No, worse. Vultures wait for their prey to die. We help 'em along here."

Slocum looked at the man, a middle-aged, balding man of considerable size. The first impression he had was one of fat. He quickly changed his appraisal when the man moved suddenly out of the way of a flying body. With easy contempt, the man reached out a huge paw of a hand, grabbed a collar, and lifted. The drunk's feet came off the floor, and he twitched weakly.

The man tossed the drunk into the arms of a bouncer. "Get rid of him, will you, Jim? And not out the front way, either. They were stacking up like cordwood last night."

"But Mr. Swan, there's not hardly any room out there now."

"Been a busy night," the man addressed as Mr. Swan said, shaking his head. "Get Frosty and Hawkins to clean it out. But don't be gone too long."

Slocum watched as Jim retreated, dragging the once-flying drunk. Along the way to the back door two bouncers joined him, one with prematurely snowy white hair and another, younger bouncer who looked as if he'd just fallen off the turnip wagon.

"Hard getting good help these days," Swan said. "Mind if I join you? That table's got a shaky leg to it." The huge man settled down, his drink on the table between them. "You want something?"

"Beer," Slocum said, deciding this was the safest thing he could drink. Whiskey could hide the taste of knockout drops.

"Hell, that's no fit drink for a man. Especially the swill I serve here." Swan gestured and the barkeep brought over a bottle. Swan poured a shot, knocked it back, then poured another into the same glass and shoved it across to Slocum.

"That'll show there ain't nothing bad in it. My personal stock."

Slocum tried the whiskey. He'd had better, but it went down smooth and didn't have the bitter taste of drugs.

"Thank you, Mr. Swan."

"Reckon it's obvious I own this saloon and cathouse," the man said, chuckling. "But then I saw you weren't the same as the others who drift in looking for a good time."

Slocum had heard all the lines in his day. He wondered what Swan wanted from him. He asked bluntly.

"No, you're not like the other customers. You're quick on the uptake and, unless I miss my guess, damned quick with that hog-leg you're packing."

Slocum moved uncomfortably, reminded that he hadn't been able to get ammunition for his Colt.

"This ain't a come-on, mister. You're hunting down someone. I know the look in your eye. Heaven above knows, I've had it often enough myself. I just don't want no trouble in here. Bill Swan's Fireproof Coffee House got a reputation for nobody getting killed in it. They might leave here a bit rumpled around the edges, maybe, but not killed permanent-like."

"I don't see the man I want. But he came in. I saw him."

"Reckon so. Most everyone in New Orleans comes through these doors at some time or another. Got what everybody wants. Good liquor, cheap and without knock-out drops in it. Girls. Got a passel of them upstairs in the cribs. Most of them don't have any disease, leastwise that I know about." Bill Swan chuckled at this. Slocum guessed the man kept the whores busy, both with customers and with his own demands. Swan was a big man. His desires might be big, too.

"What do you want from me?"

"You've got the look of someone down on his luck, but too damn proud to make a point of it. You ever do any work as a bouncer?"

"Might have," Slocum said, still scanning the crowd. "What's it pay?"

"Not as good as some places. I don't let you keep everything you take off the drunks. Half of it is mine. But the liquor's better and cheaper, too. Places like the Green Tree Dance Hall ain't worth the powder it'd take to blow 'em to hell."

"Why not?"

"They're not even safe for the damned owner, that's why. Not long ago old William Lee got himself killed dead by Bill Knuckley. Place has been passed from one owner to another ever since. This place is stable. Just me as boss. And I let the men pick out one of the girls all for himself each week as a bonus."

"What do the girls think about that?" Slocum asked.

Bill Swan laughed loudly. "You are a fine one. Never thought to ask. Reckon they like it. Don't have to playact like they're enjoying themselves. Pay's a dollar a night— and half what you get off the drunks."

"And the other benefits," Slocum finished.

"That's right. I can use a man who thinks."

"All right," said Slocum. "I'll think on it a mite."

"Can't ask any more'n that," Swan said. The huge man heaved himself to his feet and seemed to drift like a thistle across the room, dodging customers and never spilling a drop of the drink in his hand. He had left the bottle on the table for Slocum.

The whiskey went down slicker than calf slobbers, but Slocum wasn't taking too much of it. He didn't want to get blurry-eyed.

He shot to his feet when he saw the man from the *Cajun Queen* coming down the back stairs from the cribs. He reached for his six-shooter, then cursed his lack of ammunition. He'd have to take the man in some other way.

Working his way through the throng in the saloon, he pushed hard against the bar and then sidled along it. By the time he reached the back stairs, the man had reached the door into the alley where Jim and the other bouncers tossed the drunks.

Slocum paused when he saw the man reaching into his pocket. A flash of light highlighted the wallet he was drawing out.

"Chambers' wallet!" Slocum cried involuntarily. The man was using Preston Chambers' stolen wallet. The distinctive hand-tooled leather wallet had cost the gambler a small fortune in St. Louis. He'd said it was worth the expense since a man of his standing had to look the part in every detail.

Money slipped from the wallet and went into the hands of a man standing in the alleyway. Slocum shoved two drunks out of the way and got even closer, trying to see and hear what was going on.

For a moment, he thought the dark-haired man was dealing with a ghost. Money came from the distinctive wallet stolen from Preston Chambers and went to the man hidden in the alley—and it seemed that the money floated away. As Slocum worked through the crowded saloon to a spot directly behind his quarry, he saw the man in the alley.

The Negro had done his best to melt into shadow. He wore only black clothing and, incongruously, a tall black silk stovepipe hat. The money given him quickly vanished into a hidden inner pocket.

Slocum moved in, his hand touching the knife he carried sheathed behind him. This would be over quick, no matter that there were two of them arrayed against him. He had vengeance on his side and wasn't going to be denied.

He stopped dead in his tracks when he saw what the black man passed over in exchange for the money.

A dried chicken claw!

Slocum's heart skipped a beat. Chambers had died with one of those crammed into his mouth. Who was next? Who was to receive this grotesque chicken claw as a statement of death?

The black man looked up, his eyes going wide. For a

frightening moment, Slocum thought he was going to become sucked into and lost in those wide, round, hypnotic orbs. Then the black man spun away and vanished as if he had never existed.

This caused his customer to look around. Even through the crush of patrons, the burly man spotted Slocum right away. His dark eyes narrowed and his lips curled into a snarl as he went for the pistol he had stuck in the waistband of his trousers.

Slocum judged the distance across the saloon and decided he'd never be able to be sure of a clean kill if he threw his knife. Miss and he'd be unarmed.

The other man's pistol came up, centering on Slocum's body. Conscious thought gave way to instinct. Slocum did what he had to. He grabbed a saloon patrol next to him and shouted, "You son of a bitch! You can't get away with that!"

Slocum swung with all his might and connected, sending the sailor reeling backward. Two other sailors caught their mate. The level of noise in Bill Swan's Fireproof Coffee House dropped for a few seconds, then rose back to its wonted din. The other customers saw that it was only a fight in progress. Nothing unusual.

The rush of sailors to come to the aid of their mate cut off the burly man's line of sight. Slocum saw the top of the man's head as he tried to jockey for position to get in a killing shot. The surge of sailors coming to fight blocked him repeatedly.

With a snarl, the man wheeled and dashed out the rear door. Slocum was safe—on that front.

He turned and faced a tidal wave of angry, drunk sailors intent on dismembering him.

6

Slocum ducked a roundhouse punch that would have knocked his head from his shoulders. By slipping under the wild blow, however, he caught hard knuckles in the side. He grunted and tried to ride the punch. He stumbled into another sailor, who growled and pushed him back into the fray he had started.

A pair of brass knuckles tore past his face. If they had connected, he would have ended up with a broken cheek-bone—and maybe a fractured skull. Slocum took several more body blows and then sank down under the storm of punches.

What he thought to be a safe retreat almost cost him his life. Heavy boots sought to crush his face. He blocked one kick and rolled to the side. He caught several more before they stomped him senseless. Then he smashed hard against the stained oak bar. Back safe, he concentrated on keeping from being trampled.

Slocum regained his breath and worked down the bar until he got to the edge of the melee. Here he pushed to his feet and wiped sticky, warm blood from his cheek. He didn't even remember which blow had opened the shallow, bloody wound. It hardly mattered. He had escaped the battle he had started.

And he had work to do.

Leaving Bill Swan's Fireproof Coffee House, he staggered into the street and looked for a way to the back. He had to find the mysterious man who had paid money for the chicken foot. How did he get around to the alley?

Slocum straightened his ragged clothes the best he could and dabbed at the bloody smear on his face as he walked. No one paid him any heed. He was just another reveler out for a night on the town. When he found an alley he thought led around to the back of the saloon, Slocum turned cautious.

He had blundered around long enough without thinking. It was time to use his head. Slocum smiled crookedly. He had to do something different. His pistol hung empty at his side, and he wasn't in any condition to duke it out with the two farmers' burly friend.

The alley crossed the one he was interested in. Here and there along it he saw dim outlines of doors leading to shallow cellars. He had no idea what lay beneath the saloons and brothels on Gallatin Street, and he didn't want to find out. Slocum scouted the area quickly, then advanced slowly, hand on his knife.

He came to the alley where Bill Swan had his drunk patrons thrown. Several lay stripped of their money and clothes. Slocum made his way through the forest of the robbed, alert for the slightest movement around him.

Once, he spun, knife held low and the tip pointing up for a quick gutting stroke. He relaxed when he saw a sailor struggling to stand. The young salt stared at him through bloodshot eyes. His lips moved but only croaks came out.

Slocum grabbed the man by the front of his long johns and helped him to his feet.

"Did you see a black man leave here a few minutes ago?"

"No," came the weak reply. "Just a mountain of a fellow with a six-shooter in his hand."

Slocum's heart skipped a beat. This was even better. "Where'd he go? Did you see?"

The sailor pointed down the alley. Slocum let him slide back to the littered floor. He had to hurry. The man he sought had more than five minutes' head start on him.

Slocum didn't know if luck would ride with him. Such a big head start could hide an entire army in the French Quarter, much less a single man intent on not being found. He rushed out into Barracks Street and stopped to stare.

He wasn't sure if luck was the word he wanted. He had found the burly, dark-haired man. The object of his search stood in the center of the street, arms crossed and waiting for him.

The rest of Slocum's luck had turned midnight black. In a half circle around the man were a dozen thugs carrying oak staves. From the way they looked at the man in the center, Slocum knew who their leader had to be.

"You lookin' for me?" the man called out. "You lookin' for Clyde Rupert?"

"Reckon I am," Slocum said. His green eyes darted around to find a way of getting the hell away from here. He'd be floating face-down in the Mississippi River before dawn if he didn't. He couldn't fight this many men, not with them all intent on bashing his head in with their oak cudgels.

"I don't know you, but you been makin' life hard for me tonight."

"You killed my friend."

"The likes of him ain't got friends, huh, Clyde," said the man to Rupert's left. "We'll show 'em what friends are."

"Yeah, we'll show 'em," Rupert said. "The Live Oak

Boys will beat him to a bloody pulp! Get 'im, boys. Go
tear him up!"

Slocum sprinted for the relative safety of a doorway. He
had seen the iron gate open a fraction, as if the resident
inside had started to emerge, then seen the trouble brewing. Slocum didn't give the woman behind the gate time to
bolt it securely. He kicked it on the run, bowled her over,
and then spun, slamming the gate himself.

"Better get it locked. The Live Oak Boys aren't likely to
think you didn't help me," he said. He ran down a narrow
corridor and burst into a Spanish-style courtyard. Flowers
bloomed in wild profusion, and a small fountain bubbled in
the center.

He had no time to appreciate the serene beauty. Slocum
jumped onto the fountain, slipped, regained his footing,
and climbed to the top. From here he jumped, catching at
the lower rail of the second story, which looked out over
the courtyard.

Sounds of pursuit came echoing down the short corridor. The Live Oak Boys had smashed in the iron gate and
were hot after him. Slocum kicked hard and heaved himself up and over the ornamental wrought-iron railing. He
wasted no time in forcing open a window and climbing into
a bedroom. A man slept peacefully under a mosquito net.

For a moment Slocum thought he had died. The entire
room was hung in white, draped for summer in white mus-
lin. The pictures on the walls were covered, as was the
furniture. The window at the front of the room was open to
admit a weak, fetid breeze.

Slocum raced for the window and looked out into the
street below. Rupert stood in the center of the street, with
his arms crossed and the look of death in his eyes. He
directed the search for Slocum with increasing impatience.

"What do you mean you can't find him?" Rupert bel-
lowed. "*Look* for him or I'll rip out your damned eyes!"

The courtyard behind filled with the gang members.
Slocum slipped out the window when the man in the bed

began to stir restlessly. Clinging to the bric-a-brac, he edged along the front of the house. Clyde Rupert never bothered to look up or he would have seen Slocum.

Reaching the edge of the house, Slocum saw his chance. A narrow balcony on the next building afforded him a better escape route. He got the toes of his boots firmly planted against the plasterwork, then shoved hard. He flew through the air like a tattered bird. Strong hands gripped the railing. In seconds he was at the far end of the balcony and looking for another place to go.

He got to the end of the balcony and ran smack-dab into a thug carrying an oak bludgeon.

"Clyde's gonna give me ten dollars for your ears," the huge man said. He reared back to swing his club.

Slocum reacted instinctively. His hand flashed to his Colt Navy and drew it. By the time his thumb worked back the hammer to cock the six-shooter, he knew he'd made a terrible mistake. "Stop!" he shouted, trying to bluff the thug.

The Live Oak Boy was past hearing the bald lie. His face was contorted into a rictus of hate. His muscles rippled as he put every ounce of strength into the blow that would turn Slocum's face to bloody jelly.

Slocum ducked and felt the heavy stave pass overhead, taking his hat as it flashed past. In that instant, Slocum saw his opening. Instead of retreating, he attacked.

Colt shoved in front of him like a battering ram, he drove the muzzle hard into the man's midsection. Slocum followed with his shoulder, getting down under the man's center of gravity and lifting. A wild shriek greeted him as the Live Oak Boy tumbled over the railing and fell head-first to the street below.

Slocum had removed one problem only to create another: Clyde Rupert had heard the commotion and had directed his gang toward the spot where Slocum had battled so furiously. Shots rang out, knocking away bits of plaster all around him. One lead slug ricochetted off the iron railing, trailing bright blue sparks after it.

"Get him!" Rupert ordered. "Twenty dollars to the Boy who croaks him!"

Slocum ached all over from his many fights. He scooped up the fallen oak club and hurled it at Rupert. The man sidestepped with easy contempt. Slocum thought of ducking into the house and then reconsidered. The people sleeping inside were stirring. He thought he heard the action of a shotgun opening and shells being rammed into the cylinder.

Swinging out on the ironwork grille, he scampered to the roof. Bullets sent pieces of tile flying into his face as he climbed across the sloping roof. He got to the back of the house and slid down the drainpipe, then ran out the small, dark passageway leading to the street farthest from where Rupert harangued his gang.

He got into the deserted street and thought he had entered another world. Gallatin Street had been packed with drunked revelers. Girod Street saw more quiet pursuits, but only because the cribs conducted their business in low moans rather than loud singing and laughing. This street was almost funereal.

Slocum quickly saw the reason. An Ursuline convent dominated the middle of the next block. How a convent could exist so close to unbridled debauchery was something he didn't care to think about. He welcomed the cool quiet of the grounds. Slipping through like a shadow, he tried not to leave any trace of his passage.

At the gate leading back into more populous areas, he hunkered down and peered out. He thought he saw Clyde Rupert and several of his gang members but wasn't sure. Slocum took the time to rest and get his breath back.

He was still alive—and he knew the name of the man who had killed Preston Chambers. Slocum wasn't sure what good that information would do him, considering Rupert's obviously dominant position in the New Orleans underworld.

With a freshly loaded cylinder in his Colt, he'd make the knowledge into something useful. Justice was going to be done. And Slocum was going to get the money back that Rupert had stolen from Chambers.

His money.

Slocum waited another twenty minutes and decided the Live Oak Boys had moved on to other pursuits. He didn't think even Rupert could keep that gang of thugs focused for long. The lure of a twenty-dollar reward might keep them looking for a while, but none of them had appeared to be heavy thinkers.

He boldly walked into the street and retraced his steps until he got to Gallatin Street. From here he easily found Bill Swan's Fireproof Coffee House. The fracas he had started earlier had died down. Slocum went to the bar and ordered a beer. In spite of all the owner had said, Slocum wasn't pressing his luck. Warm beer wasn't as likely to hide narcotic drugs.

"You're back," came Swan's amazed comment. The muscular giant moved around and bellied up to the bar beside Slocum. "After the fight you started, I thought you'd be dead in some back alley."

"I'm resilient."

"Just like a ball of gutta-percha," agreed Swan. The man studied him carefully. "You bounce, but you're gonna get flattened real quick if you keep crossin' the likes of Clyde Rupert."

"Word travels fast," Slocum said. The beer was both warm and bitter. Still, it went a ways toward satisfying his thirst. He had been through too much this night not to appreciate it.

"I keep my ears open. That's how I stay alive and in business." Swan took a deep drink from the whiskey bottle he carried. "You'd do well to just leave New Orleans."

"The job offer's not still open?" Slocum asked.

"Not after tonight. Rupert's got it in for you bad. What'd you do to that son of a bitch?"

"Personal," Slocum said. "Doubt you'd tell me about him, even if I asked."

"Buy a bottle of whiskey and let's see."

Slocum paid five dollars for a bottle and joined Swan at the back table. To their right men wagered on fighting dogs. To the left a half-dozen men gambled at Spanish monte.

"Good choice," Swan said, helping himself to the bottle Slocum had purchased. "Damned good whiskey. Best in the Delta."

"Rupert. Tell me about him."

"You know he's the leader of the Live Oak Boys."

"A gang," Slocum said.

"More than that. They run extortion, whores, crooked gambling, just about anything in the Vieux Carré that might turn a nickel's profit." Swan chuckled. "I used to run with them. Can you believe it? I was a Boy when I was younger."

"Why'd you give it up?" Slocum asked, wondering if Swan had. He might be talking to a gang informer.

"Falling out with the former leader, before Rupert took over. By then I was just a memory and had started the Fireproof Coffee House. I don't like wandering all over town. Prefer to stay put and drink." Swan upended another glass and then poured another drink from Slocum's bottle.

"What about the man in the alley?" Slocum asked suddenly.

"What man?"

"Rupert was buying something from a black man wearing a tall silk hat." Slocum paused when he saw Swan's face. He wouldn't have thought the huge man would have been afraid of anything. He had at least six bouncers in the saloon at all times—and he was probably one hell of a brawler himself. Swan's face had gone pasty white.

"Doctor John," the saloon owner muttered.

"What about him? Rupert was buying a chicken claw."

"Bad *gris-gris*," Swan said. "Nobody talks about shit like that. Nobody."

"Not even you?"

Slocum wasn't surprised when Swan pushed back from the table and left. He had seen frightened men before. And Bill Swan was certainly that.

What was it about *gris-gris* that scared even the toughest of men in New Orleans? Slocum was sure he'd find out—if he wanted to get his share of the stolen money back.

7

Exhausted from his night's battles, Slocum found a small boardinghouse at the edge of the French Quarter to spend the night. The price struck him as exorbitant. Paying almost four dollars for lodging rankled when he wanted to conserve his money. He paid it without question, though, because the Cornstalk Inn looked clean and secure and he didn't want to spend the night with one eye open. The fine breakfast served the next morning convinced him the accommodations, although high-priced, were worth the money.

Sated and ready to track down Rupert to recover the stolen money, Slocum walked out on Royal Street and looked up and down. As before, when he had arrived fresh off the *Cajun Queen*, the street looked deserted. Not making the same mistake he had before, Slocum searched the Vieux Carré for a store selling ammunition.

He had to walk several blocks to the northeast, past Craps Street beyond St. Anne before he found a general store. He looked over their goods and considered forgetting his bag aboard the riverboat. Was it worth the effort to fetch it?

"This will do me," Slocum said when the clerk asked if he wanted anything other than the loads for his Colt.

Slocum had come to his decision. Preston Chambers' death had to be avenged. The farmers might have had a part in it: he could check them out later. A more immediate concern was Clyde Rupert. The leader of the Live Oak Boys controlled the French Quarter with an iron hand. It would be more than simple justice retrieving Chambers' wallet—and money—from a scoundrel such as Rupert.

As Slocum slid the money across the counter to the clerk, he said, "There's one more thing you might help me with."

"Sure, mister. What?"

"I'm looking for a black man—"

The clerk laughed. "Mister, New Orleans is filled with 'em. Try the docks. Look along Canal Street. Most are servants for the Cajuns and Creoles. Hell, one comes by here every now and then." This struck the clerk as uproarious.

"I'm looking for one man in particular." Slocum described the man in the stovepipe hat. The clerk's laughter died. "He might go by the name of Doctor John."

"Don't know nothing about Doctor John," the clerk said. "Get on out of here. And don't come back!"

Slocum took his time departing. Whoever Doctor John was, he instilled a fear that far surpassed that brought by Rupert and the thugs in his river gang. How could a man dealing in chicken parts cause so many God-fearing citizens such terror?

It was worth his time to find out. After all, it was apparent Doctor John and Rupert were in cahoots. The black man had supplied the chicken claw that Rupert had used aboard the riverboat.

Slocum avoided Gallatin Street on his way down to the docks. Just hanging around and keeping a sharp lookout might gain him more information than pointed questioning.

This plan didn't work too well. By noon, he was hot and sticky and had learned nothing about Doctor John. A few scattered comments had been made about the Live Oak Boys, but they weren't useful. Slocum walked to the Julia Street wharf and stared at the *Cajun Queen*.

The riverboat had been emptied of cargo. New bales and crates were slowly gathering along the dock, ready for loading in the next few days. In only six days the paddle-wheeler would be on its way back north, going to Baton Rouge and arriving in Greenville, Mississippi, two weeks after leaving New Orleans.

Slocum stared at the boat's tall wrought-iron smoke-stacks with their fancy grillwork. The side of the riverboat was being repainted in gilt and white. It shone like the mother lode itself in the bright noonday sun. Slocum had to admit that its three-hundred-foot length was impressive.

It would be all the more impressive without his bag aboard. He touched the ebony handle of his six-shooter and considered simply boarding and taking his property, but the large number of roustabouts deterred him. If he couldn't come up with the thirty dollars in another few days, steal-ing back his property might seem a fairer deal. After all, he had only Captain Stephan's word that Chambers hadn't paid the fare in St. Louis.

And Preston Chambers wasn't likely to dispute anything the officer said.

"Hey, you the pilot of this boat?" Slocum called out to a dandy strutting along the dock.

The man turned and glared at Slocum. He was dressed in dyed buckskins with dangling fringe more than a foot long. High-heeled boots had been polished so much that they had turned into leather mirrors. The man's brocade waistcoat and skin-tight emerald green breeches made him look like a circus attraction.

"Of course I am, fool," the pilot sneered. "Don't tell me you want to ship as my apprentice? Of course you do.

Everyone does." The pilot elevated his nose and turned away. "But it won't do you any good. I already have an apprentice for the trip."

"Leaving in a week?" asked Slocum.

"I should say not. We depart on the morning tide five days hence. Do get out of my way." The dandy pushed past Slocum and strutted off, master of all he surveyed.

Slocum wondered how long the finery would remain undirtied if the pilot got drunk in the wrong place. One night in Bill Swan's Fireproof Coffee House would change the pilot's appearance, and Slocum wasn't sure if it wouldn't be for the better.

He heaved a sigh. Five days—not six—before the *Cajun Queen* sailed. Time wore down on him.

He went back to Canal Street and started working his way toward the fancy mansions in the distance. Asking after Rupert got him nowhere. The mere mention of Doctor John got doors slammed in his face. Even the offer of bribes to men living by their wits got him nowhere.

He sat in the shade to consider what to do next. He left a wake of fear behind wherever he had asked about the black man with the tall silk hat. It wouldn't be long before word got to Doctor John and he came hunting for Slocum.

All in all, Slocum decided, this was what had to happen. He had to become the hunted for Doctor John.

"Why not?" he said aloud. "Rupert already wants my scalp. Why not everyone in this damned town?"

He looked up at a slender coffee-skinned woman in her early twenties. She stared at him with a combination of fear and fascination. From her dress, she was well off. Her clothing was new, clean, and, if Slocum was any judge, even stylish.

"You looking to find Doctor John?" she asked timidly.

"Can you help me?"

"It's the other way round. I'm the one needing help." She looked confused, then amended. "Not me, really. My mistress. She needs help real bad."

"Does it have something to do with Doctor John?"

"Might," the woman said. "You want to come and talk about it? That is, if you want to earn some money."

"Your mistress will pay me to find Doctor John?" Slocum's eyebrows rose in twin arches. This was a turn he hadn't anticipated. Getting paid to do what he was doing anyway would be nice—and the woman's mistress might have some idea where he could start. Slocum was fed up with batting his head against brick walls.

"She needs help real bad, mister."

"My name's John Slocum," he said, rising.

"Mine's Lottie. You want to come talk to her now? She's mighty antsy over getting word about . . ." Lottie cut off the sentence abruptly. Slocum wondered what she had almost let slip.

"Who do you work for?" he asked, walking beside the woman as she turned up Canal and worked deeper into the forest of mansions lining the street on either side.

"Mrs. Delacroix. Mrs. Constance Delacroix. A fine woman. Such things ought never happen to anyone. She's such a fine lady."

More than this Slocum couldn't get out of Lottie. The woman chattered nervously, telling him of the occupants of each house they passed. She pointed down St. Charles toward the river and almost sneered. "Americans live down there."

He started to ask if she didn't consider herself an American when Lottie supplied the answer in a roundabout fashion. "Mr. Delacroix is a Cajun and proud of it. He don't have no truck with Americans. Says they're too loud, too pushy, too rich. They don't know their rightful place."

"Tell me about Mr. Delacroix." Slocum thought this might be safer ground for the woman.

"His family's been in town going on a hundred years," she said. "Only the finest breeding. Upstanding man. The best master anyone could hope for. Even before we was set free, the Delacroix family treated us real good. Always."

"He must be very influential," Slocum guessed aloud. "Why does he need my services?"

"*He* doesn't," Lottie said quickly. "It's Mrs. Delacroix who needs you. And you got to promise to keep it quiet. She said that was real important."

Slocum nodded absently, wondering what he was getting himself into. Lottie walked on for another ten minutes, then went through an iron gate to a mansion easily as large as any they had passed. The Delacroix family was certainly well heeled.

Lottie led him around back to the servants' entrance. Slocum hadn't thought on it, but he realized he was being considered a hired hand. He shrugged it off. In his tattered and dirty clothing, he looked like a rag man. But why would a prominent society doyenne want to hire someone who looked like him?

Slocum settled down at the kitchen table. The cook offered him a glass of lemonade. He took it, sipping at its tartness until he heard Lottie's heels clicking on the parquet wood floor in the dining room. He quickly finished the drink and put it down just as she hurried back into the kitchen. Behind her came an older woman, possibly in her early forties.

Slocum appraised her just as she was sizing him up. For his part, he liked what he saw. Constance Delacroix was a lovely, almost fragile woman. Her cheeks had been lightly rouged. This contrasted strikingly with her snow-white skin. Midnight black hair was pulled back and held in place with jeweled combs. Without examining them too closely, Slocum knew the gems were real. She stood tall, her shoulders back stiffly, her chin high, and just a hint of tears in the corners of her light blue eyes.

"You have agreed to do my bidding in this terrible matter?" Mrs. Delacroix asked without preamble. She obviously found dealing with him distasteful.

"No, ma'am, I haven't," Slocum said. Her eyes widened in surprise.

"But Lottie said—"

"I agreed to talk to you. It seems we might have mutual interests. I'm not sure, since Lottie didn't tell me anything about what you want from Doctor John."

"He's not one of *them*, is he?" demanded Mrs. Delacroix. One delicate white hand fluttered like a bird to her throat. Slocum wasn't sure if he read fear or outright terror in her face.

"Mrs. Delacroix, he was *askin'* after Doctor John. Why'd he have to *ask* if he was one of his disciples?"

Slocum filed this away. Lottie spoke of Doctor John as if he were a preacher. He had never seen any preacher who wore a stovepipe hat, but then this was New Orleans. They didn't do things in the usual way here. "I'm looking for him because he had business dealings with someone who stole property of mine," Slocum said to the elegant Mrs. Delacroix.

"There's something more to your search, isn't there, sir?" the raven-haired woman asked pointedly. "I hear it in your voice. You are looking for revenge."

"Reckon so," Slocum allowed. "Clyde Rupert killed a friend of mine and stole everything he owned. Part of his poke belongs to me, since we were partners."

"Rupert?" Mrs. Delacroix shuddered. "Is he mixed up with Doctor John, too?"

"I have every reason to believe that, ma'am. But I need to know more than you're telling me. Lottie hasn't told me a thing about what you want from me."

"It's voodoo, sir. The matter is voodoo."

8

"I don't believe in such nonsense," Slocum said.

"Then you are a fool, sir. In New Orleans, belief in voodoo does matter. Voodoo is a fact of life. It *exists*." Constance Delacroix spoke with considerable passion. Slocum wasn't going to argue with the woman. Whatever had happened bothered her greatly. If she thought it had to do with voodoo, he could only listen. He didn't see how he could possibly help her.

"Maybe he ain't the one we want," Lottie suggested.

"Isn't the one," Mrs. Delacroix corrected absently. Slocum saw the tears come back to the corners of her blue eyes.

"Tell me about it. I might be able to help. Can't tell for sure until I hear your story."

"It is not a story, sir. It is the Gospel truth!"

"I didn't mean for it to sound as if I didn't believe you, ma'am," Slocum said. He wanted to get done with this as fast as he could and still be polite. Doctor John was somewhere in the city with information he needed—and Clyde Rupert had Chambers' money.

Those were debts to be paid.

"It's Mrs. Delacroix's daughter, Angelina," Lottie said, the words tumbling out. "She been—"

"Lottie, I will tell the gentleman." Mrs. Delacroix forced the word out. From his tattered appearance Slocum was anything but a gentleman. He certainly didn't look the part for sitting in a fine kitchen with the mistress of the manor. He thought Constance Delacroix might have been working on her correspondence. He saw tiny ink spots on her fingers, but if so, she dressed right fancy for writing letters. Slocum had seen women go to formal dances in less elegant attire.

"My daughter Angelina is not with us at the moment," Mrs. Delacroix said carefully.

Slocum waited for her to get to the kernel of the problem. He knew there had to be more.

"She been kidnapped!" Lottie blurted. The servant cast her dark eyes down when Mrs. Delacroix shot her an angry look. Lottie stepped back and tried to make herself vanish. But she didn't leave the kitchen. She stayed in case her mistress needed her.

"Do you think Doctor John was responsible?" Slocum asked.

"I do. He . . . he is an evil man."

"He's not good, not like Marie Laveau."

Again Mrs. Delacroix silenced her servant with a sharp look. Lottie didn't cast her eyes downward this time. She met the stare defiantly.

"We might be able to work together, then," Slocum said. "I've got other business with him."

"Really?"

"That's why I picked him, Mrs. Delacroix," cut in Lottie. "I heard him askin' around about Doctor John. He couldn't be one of his disciples if he was askin' after him."

"Very clever. Now be quiet, Lottie."

"She's right. I've got a score to settle with him. He's involved in the death of a friend of mine." Slocum hesitated to mention the chicken claw. "Several people have called the death bad *gris-gris*."

Lottie gasped and crossed herself.

"What does that mean?" Slocum asked. He had to find out more about voodoo, it looked, if he wanted to get to the bottom of Preston Chambers' murder.

"*Gris-gris* can be either good or bad," Mrs. Delacroix said, choosing her words carefully. "Bad *gris-gris* is a curse. It is a very serious matter and should never be taken lightly. You can avert bad *gris-gris* with good *gris-gris*."

"You see the wreaths on the doors?" asked Lottie.

Slocum had. He had thought they were part of some universal decorative theme.

"They drive away the bad *gris-gris*. Nothing evil can enter a house where a specially blessed wreath protects the main entrance."

"Doctor John is a voodoo master—and a master of bad *gris-gris*. He has his finger on the city's pulse and would control much more than he does, except—"

"Except that he's black," Slocum finished. His mind raced. He had seen Rupert and Doctor John together. The pair could effectively control the city. Doctor John could hold people in fear with his voodoo, and Clyde Rupert's Live Oak Boys held sway with more tangible techniques. Doctor John ruined the soul and Rupert battered the body.

The two men could run the entire city with that combination: fear and force.

"Your daughter's been taken by Doctor John? For what reason?"

Constance Delacroix turned even whiter. "I fear that Doctor John intends to use her in some vile voodoo ceremony."

"He's gonna sacrifice her!" cried Lottie. "It's gonna be awful!"

"A voodoo sacrifice?" Slocum repeated. "What do you want me to do? Rescue her?"

"Angelina's whereabouts are unknown. You must first locate her. If you can do this, there is a chance the police might free her."

"You belong to a prominent family," Slocum said. "Why don't you just go to the police and ask them to find Angelina?"

"That isn't possible," Mrs. Delacroix said. "My husband is very influential politically. This is an attempt to sway him on certain crucial matters. He has refused to give in to Doctor John's demands." She let out a tiny whimper and fought back tears. "He has refused to even approach the police about this. He claims it would diminish his power and ruin all he has been working for so long."

"But she's his daughter," Slocum said, still not understanding. "Does political power mean more to him than . . ." He cut off the question when he read the answer in Mrs. Delacroix's pained expression. Her husband did think more of power than family.

Slocum had seen it before, and he didn't cotton to it at all. Power twisted some men, even as it brought out the finer qualities in others. More often, though, the former happened.

"Deal with him, Lottie. I must go rest." Constance Delacroix spun and left the kitchen amid the rustle of her skirts. Slocum watched her leave and shared some of her pain. "There's more to it than this, it seems to me," he said to the coffee-colored servant. "Even a power-mad politician would go to the police if his daughter was kidnapped."

"Mr. Delacroix refuses to admit that's what happened," Lottie said. "He thinks Miss Angelina run off with her no-account boyfriend. He's disowned her, he says. Won't have anything to do with her. Won't even allow Mrs. Delacroix to mention her at the dinner table."

"Are you sure Angelina hasn't run off with her boyfriend?"

"No," Lottie said, eyes wide. "Doctor John's got her, and he's gonna make her a voodoo sacrifice."

Slocum wasn't going to argue with the woman. She sounded too sure of herself. "Tell me how Angelina came to be kidnapped. How long ago was it? Where? Everything you can think of might help me."

He settled down and indicated he'd like another glass of the lemonade. The tartness puckered his mouth as it erased his thirst. He listened to Lottie's tale of abduction with only half an ear.

Angelina had been sitting on the back veranda three nights ago when Doctor John's minions had crept up and spirited her away. Other than this simple fact, everything Lottie told him was embroidered truth. She went on and on about *gris-gris* and how Angelina ought to have protected herself more.

"Who is Marie Laveau?" Slocum asked suddenly. Lottie had mentioned the name before, and it hadn't meant anything to him. "Can she help in locating Doctor John?"

"Marie Laveau is a fine woman. She practices voodoo, but only to help."

"Where can I find her?"

"She wouldn't talk to you," Lottie said. "She wants nothing to do with Doctor John. They have a big fight."

Slocum nodded slowly. Even more of the power structure of New Orleans was coming to light. Marie Laveau and Doctor John were in a contest for the spiritual control of the city's populace. Even though Lottie didn't say so, Slocum figured Marie Laveau was on the outs, and Doctor John was becoming more dominant. That was the only reason Slocum could see for a voodoo queen to apparently relinquish her practice of the ancient rites.

"Where does Doctor John hang out? Is there a particular saloon?"

"Doctor John is a religious man. He don't drink. Nothing 'cept blood," Lottie said seriously.

He settled back in his chair. If he took the job, he'd have twice the headaches he already had.

"Mrs. Delacroix is willing to pay big money," Lottie said, seeing his hesitation. "Real big money."

"How big?" Slocum asked. It flashed through his mind that if the amount was more than twenty dollars, he could add the ten he still had left to it, get his bag off the *Cajun Queen*, and be headed west before sundown. Cheating Mrs. Delacroix wasn't something he'd want to do, but it would solve most of his problems.

Even if it rankled that Clyde Rupert got away with Chambers' murder, it might be for the best to just up and leave New Orleans.

"Ten dollars."

"Ten?" Slocum laughed. "That's big money?"

The look on Lottie's face told him Mrs. Delacroix had offered far more than this. The servant intended to keep whatever she didn't pass along to Slocum. "Well, that's only the part you get for taking the job," Lottie admitted.

"How much?"

"A hundred dollars."

Slocum let out a soft whistle. This was good money, but was it worth risking his neck for? He laughed aloud. He was risking his neck already for no hope of payment. Just bringing a measure of frontier justice to Rupert would be pay enough. A hundred dollars added on top would be real sweet. "I'll take the job," he said. "What does Angelina look like? Do you have a portrait around?"

"No, but you'd recognize her right off," Lottie said. "She's the spitting image of her mama." Lottie glared at him. "Don't go gettin' no ideas, Mr. Slocum. She's a good girl. She's gonna marry into a fine Cajun family one of these days, and her papa's gonna be proud of her."

"How old is she?"

"Eighteen, Mr. Slocum. And you *won't* get no ideas about her, will you?"

"I'll find her," he said. "And I'll bring her back."

Slocum finished the lemonade and accepted the ten one-dollar bills Lottie had rolled up tight and held in her hand. She made him promise to come back every day to report on his progress.

"I will need one bit of information from you," Slocum said. Lottie tipped her head to the side and waited for him to ask. "Where do you think Doctor John might be?"

"In the bayou," was all the answer he got.

Slocum felt more comfortable with his Colt loaded and ready. In his pocket he carried a spare cylinder, also loaded and ready. The gunsmith had charged him almost four dollars for the cylinder, but Slocum considered it a worthwhile investment. He wasn't going to ransom his bag from Captain Stephan with any amount less than thirty dollars. He might as well spend his cash wisely.

Outside Bill Swan's Fireproof Coffee House he saw several of the Live Oak Boys. Slocum recognized them by the oak clubs they carried. They went from one saloon to the next. It didn't take him long to figure out what they were doing—they were collecting extortion money. He heard one telling the barkeep how terrible it was to have both legs busted up, and how easy it was to pay up the ten dollars to stay well.

The bartender had paid readily.

Slocum considered robbing the trio of their ill-gotten gains. Their take for the afternoon had to be over a hundred dollars. Such a princely sum would do much to even the score with Rupert.

Then Slocum realized that only Clyde Rupert's death would truly clear the books.

Even as he came to this conclusion, he saw a black man wearing a tall silk stovepipe hat approach one of the Live Oak Boys.

"Get on out of here, nigger," the thug yelled as he waved his oak cudgel in the air. The black man seemed unafraid of the threats. He motioned again. This time the trio went into a dark alley.

Slocum hurried closer. He missed much of what was said, hearing only, ". . . in the bayous tonight. Midnight."

"Why'd Clyde want to go out there?" asked one of the thugs.

The black man said, "Doctor John wants him. You tell him that. Doctor John wants him there."

"Shit," grumbled another of the Live Oak Boys. "I don't like playin' messenger for the likes of him."

"Better do it," said the third, a nervous quiver in his voice. "You know what they can do. Bad *gris-gris*."

This simple argument sent the three rushing from the alley in search of Clyde Rupert to deliver the message. Slocum watched them go, taking their extortion money with them. He'd have no chance to rob them now, even if he wanted to.

He turned into the alley in time to see the silk top hat vanish around the corner a block away. Feet pounding, he ran after the black man. He hadn't gotten a good look at him, but this had to be Doctor John. The hat was identical to what he'd seen the night before.

Slocum rounded the corner in time to see the stovepipe hat bobbing along in the midst of a small crowd. He slowed his pace, but kept the gleaming silk hat in sight. The black man walked at a brisk clip up to Craps Street and then turned toward the river. This was a section of the French Quarter Slocum hadn't explored.

Looking around, he decided it wasn't any place to allow his quarry free rein in. The number of small portals opening to the larger courtyards would allow him to vanish without a trace.

Slocum hurried after the man and caught up with him just as he was turning down another alley. He reached out and grabbed the man's shoulder, spinning him around.

A look of surprise crossed the black man's gaunt, almost emaciated face. He pulled back from Slocum. "How dare you touch me?" he asked in a deeply resonant voice.

"Doctor John," Slocum said. "I've got business with you."

Again the surprise crossed over the thin face. "I am not Doctor John. I am not *papa-loi*. You have mistaken me for another."

"I saw you selling the chicken foot to Rupert last night."

"No, not me," the man said. A hint of fear entered his voice now. "I do not sell *gris-gris*. Doctor John doesn't allow it."

"So you've been cutting in on his racket," Slocum accused. "Do you think I should let him know about that?"

Slocum was ready for the swift movement. The black man swung away, then came back with a short, deadly knife in his hand. The blade would have found Slocum's belly if he hadn't expected an attack.

He caught the man's thin wrist and twisted hard. The knife clattered to the cobblestones. Slocum then applied even more pressure.

"You know where Doctor John is. I want to know. I want to talk with him."

"No, I cannot tell you anything!"

Slocum bent forward and drove the man to his knees. He held the bony wrist in a viselike grip. Squeezing, he felt bones begin to snap. Pain exploded on the man's face.

"You're a messenger for Doctor John," Slocum accused. "Tell me where he is and I'll let you go."

"He will kill me. He will kill *you*."

"I'll take my chances," Slocum said. This was his first opportunity to get to Doctor John, and he wasn't going to let a few threats stand in his way.

Twisting agilely, the man swung his free fist at Slocum's head. Slocum ducked to avoid the blow, letting up on the pressure on the black man's arm. Like a snake, the man slithered free and stumbled along on his knees, then got to his feet and ran as if all the demons of hell were nipping at his heels.

Slocum drew his six-shooter and yelled, "You're a dead man if you don't stop!"

His threat had no effect on the fleeing man. Slocum fired, the shot taking off the tall stovepipe hat. Still the man ran. Just as Slocum was lowering his sights for a shot to the legs to bring the man down, a loud report echoed down the alley.

Slocum thought his Colt Navy had discharged prematurely. The black man slumped into a boneless pile. Slocum stared at his pistol and realized he hadn't fired. Someone else had.

He advanced slowly along the alley, alert for the unseen sniper. He saw no one. The bullet that had brought down the fleeing man might have come from a ghost.

Kneeling, he lifted the man's head. Eyes opened and focused on him. The lips moved. Slocum bent closer to hear what the man said.

"I put a curse on you! In the name of Liba, I curse you!"

Slocum dropped the man's head to the alley, but he was dead before the head hit the dirt.

9

Slocum went to the end of the alley, expecting to be fired on with every step he took. When he got to the crossing street, he saw no one. The three blocks in either direction were deserted, as if word of another malaria outbreak had struck the area. He shoved his six-shooter back into his holster. He had been close to getting information.

If the man lying dead in the alley hadn't been Doctor John, at least he had been a trusted aide. A voodoo disciple. With a bullet in his chest, the man's loyalty had been sealed forever.

"He cursed me," Slocum said, shaking his head. "He put some kind of voodoo curse on me."

Slocum didn't believe in voodoo for an instant, but the notion still sent a cold shiver down his spine.

"There's only one way to go, if I'm going to get anywhere," Slocum said to himself. Whistling, he went in search of Marie Laveau. He stopped whistling after going less than a block. He slowed and peered into a shady cemetery. Tall white marble spires marked many of the grave sites. It took Slocum a few seconds to realize there were an inordinate number of mausoleums and tombs.

It finally hit him that the city was built behind levees—and was more than six feet under the level of the Mississippi River. To bury anyone in New Orleans meant digging down and finding water within a foot or two.

The marble crypts were the only answer, other than shipping corpses upriver to Baton Rouge or some other location.

Slocum shivered again. He preferred the notion of good, honest earth over him. He didn't want his body to molder away to dust and bone in a sealed crypt, even if it was elegant and expensive.

He turned and stopped instantly. At the intersection of the streets not ten paces away lay a decapitated chicken. His hand went to his pistol, but he didn't draw. He looked around, straining to hear the slightest sound. Slocum heard and saw nothing.

He walked over and stared at the chicken. Blood oozed from the neck stump. He looked around again, thinking the person who had left this grisly threat might show himself. No one.

Slocum scratched his chin, puzzling over how the chicken had seemed to simply appear. When he had stopped to look into the cemetery, it hadn't been in the road. When he turned back, there it was.

"Voodoo," he muttered. It wasn't anything more than an excuse to mutilate chickens. But Slocum didn't put the thong back on his six-shooter. He might not believe, but there were many in New Orleans who did, and who would do Doctor John's biding without a qualm.

He walked another few blocks, then doubled back to see if anyone was trailing him. If they were, they were quicker than he was and evaded his keen gaze. Slocum retraced his steps and found a group of children playing on the steps of a tumbledown shack.

He couldn't help contrasting this with the elegance of

the Delacroix mansion. What struck him as an even more vivid contrast was the happiness shown by the three children. They were enjoying life; Mrs. Delacroix was dreading it.

"Pardon me," he called out. "I'm lost. Can you tell me how to find Marie Laveau's house?"

One older child crossed herself. Another ran and hid. The third, perhaps nine years old, boldly walked over and stared up at him. She smiled slowly and thrust out her hand. "Tell you for a nickel."

"Seems fair," said Slocum. He fished out a dime and dropped it into the eager child's hand. "You don't have change, do you?"

The youngster shook her head.

"Then I'll have to give you a dime for the information," he concluded. This seemed to please the little girl. The other two came closer to see the shining silver coin resting in the center of the outstretched palm. When the other two children came closer, the girl's hand snapped shut faster than any bear trap.

"Rue du Rempart," she said quickly. "Can't miss it. Nice house." With that she darted off, the other two children chasing her.

Slocum watched until they vanished behind their tar-paper shack, then kept walking until he found a sign nailed to a building proclaiming this to be Rue du Rempart. He looked up and down the street and decided to head to his right. There seemed to be more houses in this direction. In the other were occasional stores.

Slocum stopped and stared at the fourth house he passed. Without knowing how he knew, he was sure this was Marie Laveau's house. A simple frame house, it had been neatly whitewashed. The yard was penned in, and a dozen chickens pecked at grain.

Closer examination showed Slocum something he puzzled over. A thick band of salt circled the house.

Slocum lifted the bar on the wood gate and went into the

yard. The chickens complained but didn't stop pecking at their corn. A large rooster saw him as a threat and came forward, head bobbing and beak stabbing out. Slocum gauged his distance, kicked, and sent the bird skidding through the dirt.

"Don't go disturbing old Jed too much," came a soft voice. "He has trouble enough with the hens."

Slocum looked up. An older woman sat in the shadows on the front porch. He had missed her when he was looking over the house. He wondered why. She was quite pretty, dressed in a worn but clean gingham dress partly covered by a new white apron. Her hair was caught up in a red silk *tignon*, giving her an exotic look.

"Never seen a woman before, son?" she asked.

"I appreciate beauty wherever I find it," Slocum said.

"My, my, now aren't you the flatterin' gentleman. I reckon I should ask you up to sit a spell. Would you care for some water? Don't have much else since the cow died last winter."

"Water would be fine."

Slocum sat on a low stool while the woman rose and went to fetch the water. She was slender and moved with easy grace. More than this, Slocum felt a presence about her. When she spoke, he had to listen.

"What brings the likes of you out this far on Rempart?" she asked, settling back in her rocking chair after getting the water. "You look as if you'd be more inclined to go a-visitin' over on Canal Street—or even out in the Garden District."

Slocum heard the hint of sarcasm in that. He knew the Creoles and the Cajuns disliked the Americans moving into the Garden District. They considered them greedy and of ill-breeding. The black woman, light in color though she was, was not of either class.

"Your sympathies lie with the Cajuns?" he asked.

"Of course they do. Since the war, things haven't been the same. Too many Yankees moving into New Orleans."

He could appreciate the sentiment. Slocum finished his water and put the glass down beside him on the porch. "I'm looking for Marie Laveau. Can you help me find her?"

The woman's eyes narrowed slightly. "Everyone knows Marie Laveau. She a fine woman. The best there is. What business do you have with her?"

"I found a chicken with its head cut off in the middle of the road not three blocks from here," Slocum said. "I thought Marie Laveau might be interested in that."

"Why? She has nothing to do with Doctor John's voodoo."

"But she is a voodoo queen. That's what I've heard."

The woman frowned. "Marie Laveau is a simple woman. She has nothing to do with voodoo."

"Do you always talk about yourself as if you were someone else?" Slocum asked.

The frown evaporated like fog in the sun, and Marie Laveau laughed. "Not much sneaks by you, does it, Mr. Slocum?"

"You seem to have a good source of information, too," Slocum said. "Was it Lottie who gave you my name?"

"The Delacroix's maid? No. I came by this information through other sources."

"What about Doctor John? Did he kidnap Angelina Delacroix?"

"I know nothing of such things. I want to know nothing. Once, these things might have interested me. No more. Not since Doctor John came here from Georgia and made himself *papa-loi*."

"I know what's happening in New Orleans," Slocum said. "I don't want the Live Oak Boys and Doctor John running the town."

"You are a drifter. You have no roots here. My family goes back a hundred years, more! What does it matter to you what happens in New Orleans?"

"You know everything that goes on in the Crescent

City," Slocum said. "You know my friend was killed on the *Cajun Queen*, his throat slit and a chicken claw put in his mouth."

"Bad *gris-gris*," Marie Laveau muttered.

"That's right, bad *gris-gris*. And I have reason to believe it was Clyde Rupert who killed him—and stole money belonging to me."

"You do not wish to anger Doctor John."

"It's too late for that," Slocum said, his temper flaring. "I was with one of his voodoo disciples when he was killed less than an hour ago. Doctor John knows me, just as you do."

"Leave New Orleans, Mr. Slocum. This is not the place for you."

"Mrs. Delacroix is upset over her daughter's kidnapping. Tell me what you can about it." Slocum hesitated to offer money to Marie Laveau. She was a proud woman. The merest hint that he was patronizing her would cut of all information. "Angelina is an innocent bystander in a desperate political power struggle between her father and Rupert—and Doctor John."

"I know nothing," Marie Laveau repeated firmly.

"I'll go," Slocum said. "But tell me, why do you have a ring of salt around your house?"

"T keep away the bad *gris-gris*," Marie Laveau answered. "Is there anything else?"

"Who is Liba?"

Marie Laveau crossed herself and muttered under her breath. "Someone cursed you in Liba's name?"

Slocum nodded.

"This is the secret name of St. Peter. It is a strong curse." She paused, then reached under the white apron over her gingham dress. She pulled out a small bag filled with an odoriferous powder. She handed it to Slocum, silently urging him to take it.

"What is it?"

"Lucky *gris-gris*. Wear it around your neck. This will keep away the curse."

"But you aren't practicing voodoo," Slocum said, tossing the bag back to her. He left the woman grumbling to herself on the porch.

Slocum walked down Rue du Rempart until he was out of sight of Marie Laveau's house, then circled and worked his way back from the other direction. She knew far more than she had admitted. The woman's eyes had widened at the mention of Angelina Delacroix.

And Slocum would have to be blind not to see her anger every time Doctor John was mentioned. There was a war brewing between the king of voodoo and New Orleans' voodoo queen, Marie Laveau.

Slocum stretched the stiffness from his joints. He had climbed into the low limbs of a banyan tree down the street from Marie Laveau's house and spent the rest of the afternoon watching. Dusk had come to blot out his view. He dropped to the ground and walked out the aches. He stopped just across the street from the voodoo queen's house.

He didn't know what he was waiting for, but when it came he would be ready.

A little after nine o'clock a carriage came rattling along the street and stopped in front of the house. Two men and a woman got out and hurried into the house. The oil lamp burning in the window of the front room winked out. In a few minutes, four people came out. Slocum was sure the addition to the party was Marie Laveau.

The carriage started off with a clatter, the single horse having a difficult time pulling the load. Slocum was able to follow at a discreet distance without having to do more than lengthen his stride. The carriage went past the Duelling Oaks and on toward Lake Ponchartrain. Just when he was sure it was going all the way to the lake, it turned abruptly and started inland again—and into the swamps.

Slocum cursed, even as he swatted at a new drove of mosquitoes making life miserable for him. He wasn't prepared for a trip into the sucking quagmire of a Louisiana swamp. He hesitated, then plunged on. He had reached his decision. If he wanted to find out Angelina's fate, he had to keep close to Marie Laveau.

She was the only one he had talked to who might know where the girl was. Slocum grinned ruefully. Marie Laveau was the only one he knew of who was still alive who might know Angelina's fate.

The carriage clattered and rattled through the night, following a dry path through the swamp. Slocum cursed his aching feet, his sore muscles, the welts from the voracious, blood-sucking mosquitoes feasting on his flesh, and picked up the pace to get closer to the carriage. He didn't want to lose the track and find himself floundering about aimlessly in the swamp.

For another hour the carriage wended its way deeper into the bayou country. Slocum began to despair that Marie Laveau was doing anything more than leading him to his death. He thought of quitting and finding his way back to New Orleans, then realized he had come too far. As his father had always told him, you don't yell "Whoa!" in the middle of the mud. He had to keep going.

He almost ran into the back of the carriage. He hadn't heard it stop or its occupants get out. The darkness enveloping him was almost absolute. The tall banyan and mango trees spread their strong limbs across the night sky—limbs draped with parasitic Spanish moss.

"We are late," the woman with the party said. "Your followers are already here, Marie."

Slocum exulted. He had been right. Marie Laveau knew far more than she had admitted. And he had followed her to a voodoo ritual in the middle of the swamps.

He advanced more cautiously, finding a thick-boled oak tree to hide behind. In a clearing stood two dozen men and women. A fire blazed in the center. On the far side a tall wooden throne had been set up for Marie Laveau. She walked toward it as regally as any European royalty and took her rightful place.

She began a chant: *He-ron mandé, tigui li papa.* Over and over she repeated the hypnotic verse. Her followers began a slow, snakelike dance around the fire. Slocum watched in utter fascination, so much so that he didn't hear movement behind him.

Only luck saved him. A dozen blacks sneaked past him, intent on the activity occurring at the fire. They failed to see him.

Another dozen moved across the open expanse to his right. Slocum held his breath, not daring to move. They didn't seem to be invited guests. He knew how accurate this guess was when he heard a cold voice from his left command, "Kill them! Kill them all!"

A black man wearing a tall stovepipe hat stepped into view. Gaunt, taller than Slocum's six-foot-one, the man held out a skeletal finger and pointed at Marie Laveau. "She dares to curse me. She dares curse Doctor John! Kill her! Kill her!"

The horde of men let out savage cries and rushed forward brandishing knives that gleamed wickedly in the firelight. Slocum saw the slaughter that would occur if something wasn't done. None of Marie Laveau's followers seemed to be armed—and many were women.

Before the first attacker had crossed half the distance to Marie's throne, Slocum stepped out and drew his Colt. He sucked in a deep breath and let it out. When his lungs were empty, his finger squeezed back. The six-shooter barked and a man died.

The man had almost reached the foot of Marie Laveau's chair when the bullet took his life. He skidded forward, face-down in the swamp.

A second shot knocked the leg out from under another man. Slocum didn't waste any time with Doctor John's minions. He swung around, his pistol looking for the voodoo leader, the *papa-loi*.

His shot went wild when a man rose up in front of him, knocking his hand off target. The bullet sang into the humid night. Slocum found strong arms circling his body, seeking his throat and eyes. He kicked hard and rolled, coming to the top of the heap.

He used the butt of his pistol to knock out his assailant. Slocum turned and tried to get a shot off in Doctor John's direction.

The voodoo leader had already stepped back into the masking darkness of the swamp, vanishing totally. The only sign that he had ever existed was the continued vicious attack by his men on Marie Laveau's voodoo worshipers.

Slocum knew he couldn't fire into the surging tide of humanity and be sure he was hitting only Doctor John's men. He quickly crossed the open space. When he got to the edge of the bonfire, he saw strangely painted faces rising up all around.

When anyone attacked, he struck back. Only once more did he fire. He wounded a man trying to knife Marie. She sat stoically, not moving. Her lips quivered, and she might have been cursing the man coming after her. Slocum couldn't tell. All he saw was that his bullet hadn't affected her attacker.

Slocum fired again and again until his pistol was empty. Each was a direct hit; one hit in the middle of the man's spine. And still the man kept up his attack.

Slocum drew his knife and savagely thrust. To his surprise, no blood spurted from the deep wound. He had hardly slowed the man's mindless attack on the woman.

Marie Laveau finished her chant. She made a motion of dismissal.

The man pushed past Slocum and ran away.

"Begone, zombie!" Marie Laveau cried. "Never return to trouble me!"

As suddenly as the attack had started, it ended. Strange inhuman wails came from deep in the bayou. Slocum thought they might be signals—but they might have been some swamp dweller complaining over disturbed sleep.

Slocum turned in a tight circle, pistol ready for action. Only those who had been here to celebrate Marie Laveau's brand of voodoo remained. Even those he had shot were gone.

"How many were hurt?" he asked.

"Only a few," came the answer from a man kneeling nearby. The man looked up and frowned. He had not expected to see a white man in the gathering.

If her followers were nonplussed over Slocum's appearance, Marie Laveau was not.

From her throne, she held out a hand. From her fingers dangled a string. Tied to the string was the lucky *gris-gris* she had offered him earlier.

"Take it, Mr. Slocum," she said. "You will definitely need it now that you have thwarted Doctor John this night."

He accepted the charm. After seeing how the man she called a zombie had taken the best he could give and still kept attacking, Slocum had the feeling she was right.

10

"I don't understand," said Slocum. He switched cylinders in his six-shooter and felt better for it. Even if Doctor John came back, he was ready for the voodoo king now.

"You shot the zombie in the back. How many times?" asked Marie Laveau. "Twice? Three times?"

"It's dark. I must have missed." Slocum didn't think he had. He had a sense about hitting a target, and the man hadn't been more than a few paces away. Even if he had struck the man squarely, he knew three bullets might not slow down a strong man. He had seen mountain men who had come into St. Louis after a winter of trapping take five and six bullets and keep on fighting.

But he *had* hit the man in the back. Three times.

"He is a zombie. He is walking undead. Doctor John dabbles in the blackest of voodoo." Marie made a face, as if she had tasted extreme bitterness and couldn't spit it out.

"Walking undead? What does that mean? The dead are dead and can't walk. I saw a cemetery full of corpses today. Not a one rose up and chased me."

"The cities of the dead," mused Marie Laveau. "Those are Doctor John's recruiting grounds. He does his evil magic and the dead rise to do his bidding. Keep the *gris-gris* I gave you. The zombies hate the smell of the powders inside."

"The dead go around sniffing at bags of dust?" scoffed Slocum.

"Thank you for your help. Many of my followers would have died without your swift gun," the woman said haughtily. "Your presence was not requested then, however, and it is not now. Go."

Slocum looked around the clearing in the bayou. The ground was dry and firm. Just a few feet in any direction it turned into a treacherous quagmire.

"I'd like to oblige, but I don't rightly think I can find my way back."

"Let him ride with us, Marie," urged a man who had been in the carriage with the voodoo queen. "He saved many lives tonight. He deserves some consideration."

"He was uninvited."

"It's a sign," chimed in the other man. "We need help fighting Doctor John. He is too strong!"

"He is *not*!" raged the woman. "There is only one leader. I am Marie Laveau. *I* am *mama-loi* of New Orleans!"

Slocum strained to hear the sounds of men over the normal swamp noises. A gator roared in the distance, and birds too numerous to identify screeched and cawed and whistled. The cacophony made it too hard for him to tell if they were alone in the bayou or if Doctor John was lurking just beyond the palè ring of fire waiting for them.

"Let's get out of here," Slocum said. "Unless you want to finish your ceremony."

"The ceremony is at an end," Marie Laveau said. She clapped her hands. Slocum blinked. Her followers faded into shadow and vanished as if they had never existed. "We return to the city. You may accompany us, Mr. Slocum."

"Much obliged," Slocum said sourly. Not having to walk through the smelly swamp suited him fine, but he didn't like the woman's pompous attitude.

Slocum had to hang on to the outside carriage rails intended for luggage. He got off on occasion to help push through the muddy spots in the road. The horse was never pleased when he got back on. Slocum thought it took twice as long to return to the city as it had to get into the bayous.

"Good night, Marie," called the man driving the carriage. He and the others vanished down Rempart Street, leaving Slocum and Marie Laveau in front of her house.

"You have done a great service for me tonight," she said. She heaved a deep sigh, as if she'd come to a momentous decision. "Come into my house. I will tell you many things about your Angelina Delacroix."

This took Slocum by surprise. The woman had been silent during the entire trip back to New Orleans. He hadn't expected any cooperation at all from her.

He followed her to the front porch. She motioned for him to stay. The woman returned a few minutes later with glasses of water. She handed one to Slocum and drank deeply of the other.

"I am an old woman," she said. "I am too tired to fight Doctor John."

"You're not an old woman," Slocum said. "And it didn't look as if you're the least bit shy about locking horns with Doctor John."

"I have four children," she said. "My husband is dead of the malaria. I have a . . . patron who cares deeply for us, but I refuse his charity."

"Patron?"

"I once was the belle of the octoroon ball. Monsieur Charles is a very kind man."

Slocum said nothing. The well-to-do Creole and Cajun men often chose their mistresses at the weekly octoroon ball, a parade of only the loveliest café-au-lait women. He could see where Marie Laveau would have been a stand-out. Fifteen years earlier, very few would have been able to hold a candle to her. Even now, she had a dignity and ethereal beauty that could turn any man's head.

"They call me a witch. Some call me far worse names. But my voodoo is important. I help those who need it. And never have I cast a spell to injure. I am not like Doctor John. He sells his wicked charms. He works evil."

"What about Angelina? What does Doctor John have against her?"

"He has nothing against her. She is a pawn, nothing more. He fights her father for political control of New Orleans. You have the clear vision. You see what is happening in this city. Clyde Rupert and Doctor John have joined forces to seize control of everything."

"I had the impression that the Live Oak Boys controlled the dock area."

"They do. They work up and down Gallatin Street, also. Murder, arson, extortion, these are only some of the crimes they use to instill fear."

"And Doctor John works on the religious side, taking away your followers."

"He takes nothing away from me."

"He subverts the good you try to do," Slocum said, looking for the key to unlock the information he needed from the woman.

"He does. It was he who kidnapped Angelina Delacroix. The gossip is that he spirited her away from her own porch, in the earshot of her family."

"Her father thinks she ran off with a no-account boyfriend."

"She has no lover. She is Cajun. The family would never be more than an arm's length away should a possible suitor call on her." Marie made a hissing sound like a snake. "This is Oram Delacroix's way of denying Rupert's hold over him."

"How does Delacroix oppose Rupert and Doctor John?"

"He is rich and has considerable influence among the

Cajuns. Money and power go hand-in-glove," Marie La-veau said. "Rupert tries to take the power away. He is not of good breeding, and this offends Oram Delacroix, as it should." She shrugged. "Such a battle was inevitable. If not between Delacroix and Rupert, then among others."

"Doctor John kidnapped Angelina," Slocum prompted. "What did he do with her?"

Marie Laveau laughed, but it was a sound totally without mirth. "The rumors are that he plans to use her as a human sacrifice in his voodoo ceremonies. I do not doubt it. However, he has done something far worse with her."

"Worse than killing her?" Slocum couldn't imagine what this might be.

"She is from a proud and noble Cajun family. Doctor John put her in one of Rupert's brothels."

"What!"

"He sells her like a common whore."

"Does Oram Delacroix know?" asked Slocum. Publicly, the girl's father might say she'd been whisked away by a boyfriend, but a man of his connections had to have heard the truth.

"He might. He might refuse to listen to anyone about Angelina. If he does know, he is the kind who would think it better that his daughter be dead. Such disgrace is not to be borne."

"Which whorehouse is Angelina being kept in?"

"There are several. I cannot say for certain." Marie finished her water and silently pointed to Slocum's glass. He shook his head. It was more important learning where Angelina Delacroix was being held prisoner and doing something about it.

"Which ones might she be in?"

"Basin Street has several you might search for her." Seeing that Slocum wasn't familiar with the area, she said, "From St. Peter Street in the Vieux Carré south to Canal and over to Toledano Street. That is where the whores are to be found."

"Canal Street?"

"Yes, there are whores and there are . . . whores."

Slocum didn't ask her to explain this cryptic statement. He listened intently while Marie Laveau told him of Josephine Killeen's house on Basin Street and Clara Fisher's brothel on Phillipa Street.

"And if she is not at either, there is Katherine Cunningham's den of iniquity at Number Forty Basin Street."

"I'll start on Basin," Slocum decided. "The chances for finding her seem greater there."

"Do not take off your lucky *gris-gris*," Marie Laveau said. "Remember the zombie. Remember that you cannot kill those who are already dead."

Slocum snorted at this, but touched the bag dangling around his neck. It was pure superstition—but he saw no harm in wearing the bag, just for a while longer.

Slocum saw that he wasn't likely to be accepted as a client in Katherine Cunningham's establishment. He wasn't properly dressed for a night on the town. The men coming and going through the front door were well off. He wasn't sure if it was any benefit for Angelina Delacroix to be sold into whoredom at a high-class brothel.

How many of the men visiting this place recognized her—how many insisted on her, even as they vocally disclaimed any knowledge of who they bedded? Oram Delacroix had influential friends, of that Slocum was sure. He also had made powerful enemies. What price would they pay to disgrace the Delacroix family through its captive daughter?

The house filled most of a block. He peered through the door every time it opened and saw there was a suite of rooms on the common street side. Mantels and fireplaces of white marble gleamed in understated elegance, contrasting with black walnut furniture. As far as Slocum could see, there were velvet carpets and plush damask everywhere inside. The large plate-glass doors were gilt-edged and were guarded by two burly bouncers.

Only the finest of New Orleans society entered these doors.

And he had no idea if Angelina Delacroix was inside.

"Pardon, sir," Slocum said, stepping up to a well-dressed man leaving the brothel.

"I don't give handouts." The man jerked away and started to walk in the other direction.

"I'm not asking for one. I just wanted some advice."

"Advice?" The man frowned. "Get a job. Be productive." He started off again.

"Not on that, sir. I . . . I'm rather well off. Shipping and all that," Slocum lied. "I just don't want my friends to see me down here."

"There is nothing wrong with Mrs. Cunningham's establishment. It is among the finest in New Orleans."

"I understand that. I'm looking for something . . . special. Dark-haired, young—and she must have blue eyes. That is a necessity."

"I begin to see," the man said. He winked broadly. "Mrs. Cunningham has just the item for you, sir." He touched the brim of his hat and sauntered off.

Slocum slumped. He had checked out the other brothels and had drawn a blank. Clyde Rupert and Doctor John had sold Angelina to the finest whorehouse on Basin Street—and the hardest for Slocum to enter. He needed finery to be able to walk in without arousing any furor at the door.

He had to take another course to getting her free. Slocum walked around the block, scouting the possibilities of entering the whorehouse without being seen. They didn't look good. The doors leading into the house from the upper balconies were protected by wrought-iron grates. The few exterior doors, the one with the plate glass and two others leading to the inner courtyard, were secured by guards.

Slocum found a drainpipe in a back alley and scrambled up it. He swung onto the tiled roof and edged along until he could swing over and onto the balcony facing Basin Street.

He pressed his back against the wall and hoped that no one in the street below noticed him. At this time of night, most houses in New Orleans saw their occupants sitting on the upper balconies, partaking of the soft breezes. Not so in this house. All the activity went on inside.

Pressing his face against one window, Slocum peered into an empty room. The furnishings were every bit as fine as those in the sitting room downstairs. From deep in the house came the sounds of a piano playing. A rich contralto voice started singing. Mrs. Cunningham even provided first-rate entertainment for her patrons.

Slocum moved along, looking in one window after another. The third window was open to admit the moist breeze blowing off the Mississippi River. In the bed a man and a woman wrestled passionately. The woman's moans of joy carried to him.

He moved on. The next window gave him a view into a room where a woman sat facing a vanity mirror. She listlessly brushed her long, dark hair. The only light in the room came from a guttering oil lamp on the bedside table. Slocum tried to get a better look at the woman. The hair color was right—it was identical to Mrs. Delacroix's. But was this Angelina?

Slocum took a deep breath. There was only one way to find out.

"Angelina!" he called. "Angelina Delacroix!"

The woman turned. Shadows hid her face and kept him from positively identifying her. But from the set of her shoulders, he thought this was the young woman he sought.

"I've come to free you!"

Before she could answer, he heard the squeaking of rusty hinges. Slocum looked to his right. A huge man carrying an oak club pushed through the wrought-iron door and came out onto the balcony.

"You fuckin' pervert!" the bouncer growled. "I'm gonna smash your brains all over the street!"

Slocum had no more time to ask after Angelina Delacroix. He found himself fighting for his life.

11

The oak cudgel crushed into the ironwork with a resounding *crash*! Slocum barely ducked out of the way of the rebounding wooden club. The man using the weapon knew how to make the most of it and kept Slocum on the defensive.

"Pervert. Peepin' in ladies' windows!" The man rushed Slocum, wood shaft used as a battering ram now. Slocum caught the butt end of it in the stomach. He felt air gushing out of him as he stumbled backward. Only his large silver belt buckle kept the oak rod from doing real damage to his belly.

Slocum kept backing up as fast as he could, but the bouncer came on like a runaway steam locomotive. Huffing, puffing, grunting, the man was intent on turning Slocum's head into bloody pulp with the wooden bludgeon he swung so easily.

Slocum's fingers touched the ebony butt of his Colt Navy, but the club crashed down on the back of his hand. Seering pain shot up his arm. He knew he wouldn't be able to close the hand around his six-shooter, much less use it effectively now.

"You're dead meat," cried the mountain of a man towering above him. In the street below, several curious onlookers watched the fight with some interest. Slocum thought he heard one enterprising gambler taking bets on how long it would take for the bouncer to kill the intruder.

Slocum wanted to put a bet down—and he had more to win than just a few dollars. His life hung in the balance.

Falling hard, he lay on his back and waited. The bouncer rushed him, oak stick raised for the kill. Slocum twisted to his side, one foot going behind the man's ankle and the other snapping out hard against his kneecap. The loud pop as the kneecap shattered rivaled the sound of the oak club splintering against the ironwork.

The bouncer teetered for an instant, then screamed and fell over the railing, his right leg useless. He landed headfirst in the street. Slocum peered through the ornate ironwork. From the crazy angle of the man's head, he had broken his neck when he hit.

Slocum scuttled like a crab to the end of the balcony. Inside the brothel he heard other guards coming. To stay now was to die. He still couldn't close his right hand, and fighting another mountain of gristle and meat was out of the question.

He slithered over the end of the balcony and dropped to the street. The impact rattled his teeth, but he hardly noticed. He was off and running, making it around the corner and out of sight before any of the men from the high-priced whorehouse could pursue.

Slocum slowed his breakneck pace, then stopped to catch his breath. He massaged his right hand until feeling returned. It throbbed, but he didn't find any broken bones. He winced as he flexed the fingers, but the action made them feel better.

"So much for that," he said to himself. Subterfuge

hadn't worked. He would have to try a frontal assault. After the commotion he had just caused, this would be the last tactic anyone inside would expect.

He knew he had another advantage. No one knew who he was. They might think he was just another Peeping Tom and not someone intent on stealing away their star attraction.

What rankled the most was that Slocum wasn't even sure if the woman he had called out to was Angelina Delacroix.

Slocum slipped into a dark alley and waited. Ten minutes passed, then a half hour. Several men strolled by, out for a night on the town. He bided his time. The right victim would present himself eventually. More than an hour passed before Slocum saw his free ticket into Mrs. Cunningham's whorehouse. The man strutted along, swinging a gold-headed cane. The gray silk top hat he wore shone in the light from the gaslights down the street, and his pearl gray cutaway fluttered slightly in the evening breeze.

He took one step past Slocum's hiding place. He didn't make a second. Slocum swung his pistol and connected squarely with the back of the man's head. Like a pole-axed bull, the man crashed to the street. Slocum struggled to pull him into the dark alley and out of sight of any passing police. The whole time he had been waiting for someone to come by Slocum hadn't seen any lawmen, but he wasn't taking any chances. New Orleans might be a wide-open city, but a run-in with the law now would ruin his chances of rescuing Angelina.

The fancy dress coat fit a bit snugly across Slocum's shoulders, and the man's trousers were loose in the waist. Slocum cinched up his gunbelt to hide the ill-tailored look. He checked the man's wallet and scowled. For someone this well-dressed, Slocum had expected him to be carrying more money. Less than twenty dollars rested in the wallet. Slocum put the money he had left in the wallet, then paused.

Almost forty dollars. He needed only thirty to get his bag back from Captain Stephan. Why risk his life to rescue Angelina Delacroix? This wasn't any of his business. Zombies, voodoo, political squabbles—none of it was his concern.

The promise of another ninety dollars from Mrs. Delacroix was hardly enough to keep on if he'd get his head bashed in by one of Rupert's Live Oak Boys. He closed the wallet and slid it into the inside coat pocket. He'd made up his mind.

He had to get Angelina Delacroix out of the cathouse. If everything he'd heard about the woman was true, she was a victim of circumstance as much as he was. He hadn't asked for Preston Chambers to be murdered and his money stolen. Angelina hadn't asked to be kidnapped as part of a voodoo sacrifice scheme.

Slocum walked past the body of the bouncer still lying in the street. No one bothered to remove the now stiff corpse. The man at the door was watching him closely; Slocum sneered slightly at what an upper-class gentleman would consider an unsightly advertisement for the whorehouse.

"You really ought to clean that up," he said as he pushed past the bouncer. The man started to stop him. Slocum handed him a ten-dollar greenback as if the gesture meant nothing to him.

He heaved a sigh of relief when the man held the plateglass door open and said nothing. Slocum had passed the Cerberus dog guarding the entrance to Hades. The trick now lay in escaping this hell with Angelina Delacroix.

Inside, the brothel was everything Slocum had imagined from his brief glimpses from outside. Soft couches lined the walls. Fine oil paintings hung on the walls. The music from the piano in a back room gave just the right note of refinement.

"Good evening, sir. We haven't seen you in our establishment before," greeted a young woman. Slocum had to study her for a moment before realizing what was out of place. The bottom of a lewd tattoo crept out from under the sleeve of her fine velvet gown. "I'm Mrs. Cunningham, the proprietor."

"Good evening, ma'am," he said in his most genteel manner. "I'm newly arrived in the Crescent City. From St. Louis. A friend there had recommended your establishment to me and, having a few minutes to spare, I decided to come by."

All the time he was talking, his keen eyes studied the layout. For all the expensive furnishings, the brothel was an armed fortress. No fewer than six armed guards circulated through the interior. Any fuss he might raise would be answered quickly—too quickly.

"What is your friend's name?" the woman inquired.

"Doesn't matter," Slocum said brusquely. "Might I get a drink? I've got quite a thirst."

"Of course, sir. This way, please." Mrs. Cunningham led the way to the back room where the piano player tapped on the keys and a woman sang. The instant he entered the room, Slocum's heart jumped to his throat. Seated at the far side was Clyde Rupert.

Would the leader of the Live Oak Boys recognize him? Slocum didn't want to give him the chance.

He turned toward the woman and said, "Anything will do. Whiskey. Here, my dear. For you." He passed over another of the ten-dollar-bills. What remained in his wallet were smaller-denomination bills. He hoped that he didn't have to put out any more. The woman might get suspicious that a man as well-heeled as he pretended to be carried crumpled one-dollar bills.

Slocum turned and followed her, keeping his back to Rupert. Straining, he heard the thug saying, ". . . keep her for another few days, then let Doctor John have her. Might use her myself again. She's got fire, that one does."

Slocum's hands clenched. He knew whom Rupert spoke of. It made rescuing Angelina even more imperative.

"Here, sir," Mrs. Cunningham said. "Your drink."

"A fine place you have here," Slocum, said, more interested in keeping his back to Rupert than talking with the madam.

"It cost more than a hundred thousand dollars for the building," she said proudly. "The furnishings cost over forty thousand."

"And well worth it," Slocum said. He cleared his throat. This charade was wearing on him. "I am interested in something . . . special," he said in a low voice.

"Indeed, sir," teased Mrs. Cunningham. "Am I special enough?"

"More than special," Slocum said solemnly. "However, I have a certain preference. For dark-haired Cajuns. The young ones, especially—but not *too* young. I prefer an innocence in my women, but not *too* innocent." He struggled to think of a better way to frame his request.

"I have just the lady for you, but she is more expensive than the others."

"Doesn't matter," Slocum muttered, turning again as Clyde Rupert passed within a yard on his way out of the room. "Money is no concern, except that I must see the lady first."

"We can certainly oblige."

"So bring her here!" Slocum said.

What Katherine Cunningham said next thrilled him. He had, indeed, found Angelina Delacroix.

"She does not leave her room. She is like a hothouse flower, protected and cherished. Come along, sir. Bring your drink. I am sure she will pleasure you."

"I'm sure," Slocum said, following the woman up the stairs. He closed his eyes and tried to estimate which room he'd seen the woman he thought to be Angelina through the window. It was just about the room where Mrs. Cunningham stopped and unlocked the door. She coyly dropped the key, which was tied to a long black grosgrain ribbon, into her bosom.

"See if she appeals to you."

Slocum looked into the room. Angelina Delacroix looked exactly as Constance Delacroix must have looked twenty years earlier. Sad blue eyes stared at him, eyes haunted and hollow at the same time.

"She will do," Slocum said.

"The price is fifty dollars."

"Right here," Slocum said, drawing his six-shooter. He cocked and aimed it. "Inside. Now."

She tried to scream. He clamped his hand over her mouth. He cursed when the madam bit him. Roughly, he shoved her into the room and slammed the door.

"Let out even one peep and you're dead," he said. The coldness in his voice paralyzed the woman. She stared at him, as if she had never seen his like before.

"What do you want from me?" asked Angelina. She rose and began unfastening her bodice.

"Not that," snapped Slocum. "Tie her up. We're getting out of here."

"You won't get ten feet from here," threatened Mrs. Cunningham. "You don't know who you're crossing."

"I saw Rupert downstairs. You've got it backwards. He doesn't know who *he's* crossing," Slocum said. This stunned the woman and gave Angelina the chance to put a gag in the woman's mouth.

"Who are you?" asked Angelina. "Did my papa send you?"

Slocum made sure the madam was securely trussed up and tied on the bed. He glanced out the window. A guard sat at the far end of the balcony. His earlier excursion along this route had alerted them.

"We'll talk about that later. Do you know any way out of here?"

"Down the hall. There's a private stair at the back," said Angelina, more animated now. She paused just outside the door to the room that had been her prison. "This isn't some cruel joke, is it? Mr. Rupert does terrible things to me."

"If I saw Clyde Rupert right now, I'd put a slug between his eyes," Slocum told her. "Let's get the hell out of here and we can compare how much we hate the son of a bitch."

Angelina hurried down the corridor and paused at the door leading to the stairwell. She looked back toward her room, as if she felt guilty about leaving. Slocum pushed her roughly down the first few steps, then she regained her balance and hurried along without his goading.

"I can't believe it," she said. "I just can't. It seems like I've been a prisoner here forever."

"Hush," Slocum said, pressing his ear against the door panel at the foot of the stairs. He heard men talking outside.

"There's no other way out that I know," Angelina said. She ran her hands through her raven's-wing dark hair in a gesture of complete frustration. "They'll do terrible things to me again. I tried to escape twice before. They . . . they punished me." She shuddered as if she'd come down with the ague.

"We're leaving," Slocum said, making a quick decision. The young woman was falling apart in front of him. He couldn't hope to escape with her if she lost her courage.

Slocum drew his Colt and jerked open the door, ready to get the drop on the guards outside.

He had expected two men. He faced five.

12

"Live Oak Boys!" cried Angelina Delacroix. She tried to turn and run. Slocum grabbed her arm and swung her around hard.

The men in the alley were more startled to see Slocum and Angelina than he was to find them waiting. He had expected a pair of thugs to be on guard. Three extra only gave him a more difficult escape than he'd counted on.

His six-shooter barked once, twice, a third time. Slocum didn't aim to kill: he wanted to put fear into their hearts. Two of his lead slugs hit men in the upper leg. They went crashing down like giant redwoods felled in a California forest. Their thrashing bodies caused an obstacle for two more.

And the third Live Oak Boy caught Slocum's bullet in the middle of his chest.

The man looked down stupidly at the small hole. A red circle began to expand. He touched it almost gingerly, then said in a shaky voice, "He shot me."

The confusion this simple statement caused gave Slocum the chance to jerk hard on Angelina's hand and drag her into the alley. By the time they had run a few yards, the last thug Slocum had shot was bellowing at the top of his lungs for a doctor.

"Confusion to our enemies," Slocum told Angelina, smiling. He pulled up abruptly when they reached Basin Street. They would be noticed instantly if they continued to run. From the alley came a soul-tearing ululation that reminded Slocum of a trapped coyote.

"The Live Oak Boys' danger call," said Angelina. "There'll be a dozen of them here in a few minutes."

"Then let's not walk." Slocum hailed a passing carriage. The driver pulled over and Slocum pushed Angelina in before him. He gave the driver two of his hoarded greenbacks and snapped, "Up Canal Street."

The driver took off at a steady clip, the horse's hooves clattering loudly on the cobblestones. Angelina grabbed Slocum's arm hard and asked, "Where are you taking me?"

"Home," he said. He couldn't understand her fright. She let out a yelp of fear and shoved hard against him. Slocum rocked to one side in the carriage. Angelina took the opportunity to jump from the far side. She hit the street running.

"Son of a bitch," cried Slocum. He handed the driver another of his precious greenbacks, then rushed after Angelina. He caught her just as she was starting down Bourbon Street, going into the heart of the Vieux Carré.

He caught her arm and swung her around to face him. "What are you doing? I'm taking you home!"

"No," she said.

Slocum started to demand an explanation when he saw two men coming down the street. Both carried long oak staves. And both men had spotted Angelina.

"In here," he said, roughly shoving her into a doorway. The door leading into the courtyard of the house was securely locked. Try as he might, Slocum couldn't budge it.

"What's wrong?" Angelina asked.

"We've got to get out of here. Two of Rupert's men are coming down the street, and they must have spotted you."

Slocum had no more time to find out. The hoodlums stopped in front of the door. One was saying to the other, ". . . around here somewhere. Couldn't have vanished into thin air."

Slocum never gave either of them time to react. He stepped out, his pistol swinging. He clipped one behind the ear. The thug dropped as if every bone in his body had turned to mush. The other sensed the attack coming and was getting ready for it. His oak club was swinging.

Ducking, Slocum let the weapon knock off his fancy hat. He drove his left fist as hard as he could into the man's exposed midriff. When the ruffian doubled over, Slocum kicked him squarely on the chin. The man's head snapped back, and he fell across his friend.

"We've got to get out of sight. They must be everywhere."

"I thought I saw some patrolling Canal."

Slocum shook his head. He should have known Angelina's reaction in the carriage was based on fear of Rupert's men. He just hadn't let her explain.

"If you see any more of them, let me know. Don't go running off."

"All right," she said contritely. "Where are we going?"

"I wish I knew," he said. They hurried along Bourbon Street, the saloons and dives becoming more frequent. There wasn't any good place to hole up and wait for Rupert's wrath to die down. Slocum turned toward the docks. There might be some shanty they could use until the Live Oak Boys got tired of hunting them down. Along the river would be the last place Rupert would think to look.

"We're going into the heart of their territory," Angelina complained. She pulled away from him, still suspicious. Slocum explained his tactic. She subsided, still not convinced.

They entered the Place d'Armes. On either side

stretched the Portola, housing that Slocum knew he could never afford. But just off the plaza was a burned-out husk of a building.

"What was it?" he asked Angelina, pointing out the derelict house. "What happened there?"

"I don't know. It's not far from the market. I seem to recollect hearing about a fire in the neighborhood a few weeks ago."

"Let's take a look." Slocum pulled her along, acutely aware of anyone looking in their direction. No one he thought might be with the Live Oak Boys came near, though anyone might be an informer. He stepped across the charred threshold of the house and started into the ruins.

"Here," he said after ten minutes of searching. He heaved open a trap-door. Most houses in New Orleans didn't have cellars, owing to the high water table; this was hardly what he'd call a proper root cellar.

"It's dark down there," Angelina said fearfully.

"I'll find a lamp and get some furniture." He had already spotted a mattress and lamp. The lamp had only a few drops of oil in it, but it would do to quiet Angelina's nerves. Slocum scouted the area and didn't see anyone taking any interest in them. He crowded back down into the narrow cellar, having to crawl on hands and knees.

"This is better," Angelina said, crawling onto the mattress. "And light! It's wonderful." She shivered in spite of the sultry night air that crept down through the smoky ruins above them. She let out a sigh of pure relief when Slocum lit the lamp and sloshed the coal oil around a bit. It wouldn't burn long, but it would serve its purpose in calming the young woman's nerves.

Slocum looked at Angelina Delacroix as she lay back on the mattress, at peace for the first time since he'd rescued her. She looked like her namesake—an angel come to earth. Her hair floated above her head and spread out on the dusty mattress in a dark fan. Pale skin gleamed like alabaster in the dim light from the lamp. Never had Slocum seen a woman more beautiful or desirable.

She opened her eyes. The blue orbs locked with his. "You saved me," she said softly. "I owe you more than I can ever repay."

"It's not necessary," he said. "Rest up. We'll get out of here when the coast is clear."

"I owe you,' she repeated. Slender fingers reached out and touched his cheek. "You're not like the others, nothing like the men they sent to me."

Slocum wanted to tell her to stop, that there wasn't any debt she had to pay. But the Cajun woman's beauty took away his words and will. He bent and lightly kissed her on the lips.

The kiss deepened. Slocum knew he was lost. Even if he wanted to do the decent thing, the honorable thing, he wasn't going to be able to. And Angelina Delacroix didn't want him to. Her fingers worked through his lank black hair and stroked across his shoulders.

He moved closer, his body pressing into hers. She took the initiative by unfastening his gunbelt and helping him work free of his fancy stolen coat.

"You don't have to," he managed to say between kisses.

Angelina breasts heaved up and down. She looked at him squarely and said, "I want to. I want to see how it is because it's right, not because they're forcing me."

Slocum began unfastening the bodice of her dress. The laces came away easily, exposing the twin mounds of her creamy breasts. He caught one up in his hand, stroking softly, tugging harder when he got to the nipple. The tiny button hardened with lust.

He popped it into his mouth and sucked. Angelina gasped with pure pleasure. Her back arched, and she began writhing on the mattress.

"More," she sobbed out. "I want more. I want it all! Do it to me. Please!"

Slocum shifted his oral attention to her other breast. His

tongue licked across the penny-colored tip until he felt her heart throbbing through it. Then he kissed upward, finding her swanlike throat. At the hollow, he tongued and kissed. She was moaning constantly now, rubbing her body against his.

"Got to get more clothes off," he muttered. As he moved to strip off his shirt and trousers, she began where he had left off.

Her ruby lips found the tip of his chin, the hollow of his throat, the tangled mat of hair on his broad chest. She kissed and licked and lightly nipped as he struggled in the cramped space to kick out of his trousers.

"What's this?" she said, helping him slip the loose trousers off his hips. She gripped his erection hard and squeezed. Slocum thought he'd lose control then and there.

"It goes here," he said, reaching up under her light skirt and finding the furry triangle of her sex. His finger plunged into her moist, yearning cavity. Together they both gasped in delight at the manual intrusions.

Angelina began stroking up and down his length until Slocum thought he was going to explode like a stick of dynamite. He cupped both her breasts in his hands and began rotating them, slowly at first and in the same direction. When he changed directions, going clockwise with his right hand and counterclockwise with his left, she lifted her hips off the mattress and rubbed her crotch against his leg.

"I can't stand it," she moaned out. "I need more. Give me more. Please!"

He rolled atop her. The young woman's thighs parted softly. He edged upward, the tip of his shaft touching her nether lips. He felt her excitement. She trembled like a leaf in a high wind.

"Now. Now!" she cried. Her hips rammed down far harder than Slocum would have thrust. She impaled herself totally on his massive length. Then she began grinding her hips, driving him even deeper into her humid center. He felt the walls of female flesh clamping down powerfully around him, a gold mine threatening to collapse and crush him.

This was the way he wanted to die!

He began pulling back. She locked her heels behind his back, trying to hold him in. He retreated until just the purpled crown of his fleshy, aroused pillar rested within her. He paused for a moment, then slid forward quickly. The friction warmed him—and set the Cajun woman on fire.

Her long legs tensed and pulled him deep into her. He began moving in a slow circular motion, stirring her to even greater heights of passion.

Slocum kissed her full on the lips, then moved back along the line of her delicate jaw and lightly nipped at her earlobes. Her fingers clawed along his back as the fury of her passion rose to the breaking point.

He began stroking slowly, methodically, wanting to get the most out of the lovemaking as possible. Angelina urged him to greater speed, deeper penetration, more, *more*!

His control began to fade, and his hip movements turned jerky. He began stroking faster, finding a rhythm that ignited both their loins from smoldering fervor to passionate fire.

Slocum felt the tingling at the bottom of his balls. It spread slowly at first, then filled his lower body. He drove harder and harder into the woman, trying to split her apart with his fleshy sword. The hot tide of his rising seed erupted and spilled into her.

Angelina gasped and shoved her hips downward, trying to get even more of him into her body. She shivered deliciously and then let out a long, low sigh.

"I've never felt like this before," she said in a tiny voice. "I didn't know it could be this good. I had an idea it might, but—"

"You started all wrong," Slocum said, not wanting to remind her of her imprisonment.

"It doesn't matter how it happened. It did."

"You're all right now. We'll get you home and—"

"No!"

"Why not?" he asked, confused. "When they've stopped looking for us, we can—"

"No!"

Angelina took a deep breath and turned from him, her back resting along his chest. The soft curve of her behind fit neatly along the curve of his body. He put his arm around her.

She shrugged it off. "I can't go home. I've been disgraced."

"It wasn't your doing."

"Papa would kill me. I have shamed the family. I am a disgrace. You don't know how it is."

"Your parents wouldn't—"

"They would!"

Slocum saw there wasn't any reasoning with her. He moved away to let her rest. She might reconsider—she had to—when she had rested and the captivity was behind her.

Slocum dozed off, stirring now and then in the hot night. A ray of light slanted down through the spaces in the floor over his head. He sneezed and stretched. It was morning and time to get Angelina back to her family. He rolled over to awaken the woman, but she was gone.

13

Slocum scrambled into his clothes the best he could in the tight space. He checked his Colt before wiggling out of the partial cellar and into the bright light of a shining New Orleans day. The clouds that had threatened to dump sheets of rain on the city for days had cleared, leaving the sky a sharp, crystalline blue. Here and there floated a few white clouds. Other than this, there wasn't anything to stop the intense beating of the sun.

Slocum broke into a sweat before he got to the edge of the burned-out house. Not far away men and women were making their way to the old French Market to buy and sell produce. He tried to decide where Angelina was most likely to have gone.

He drew a blank every time he thought on it.

"Why'd she leave me like that?" he wondered aloud. Then he realized that she had meant it about Oram Delacroix's wrath. Her father would do worse things to her than Clyde Rupert and Doctor John ever had. To be Cajun and ostracized by your family was the worst possible punishment. Slocum cursed anew. None of this was Angelina's fault. If anyone was to blame, other than Rupert and the voodoo priest, it was Angelina's power-hungry father.

His political ambitions burned too bright. He was willing to trade a daughter for ever more control in New Orleans.

Slocum started searching for the young woman near the docks. He ducked out of sight several times when he saw men walking along, swinging the oak sticks that were their badge of authority. Rupert's Live Oak Boys had the entire dock area under tight control. He didn't doubt that Doctor John's grip on the French Quarter was as firm.

The city was too big for him to search aimlessly. Slocum turned from the docks and went to the Place d'Armes, hoping to find someone who might have seen her.

There were large numbers of street vendors, but Slocum didn't dare stop and ask. He had no idea which were informers for the Live Oak Boys and which weren't —or if anyone in New Orleans wasn't under Rupert's thumb.

He knew one man who wouldn't be. He headed for Bill Swan's Fireproof Coffee House. The saloon was almost deserted at this time of day. The workers taking a break for lunch had yet to come in. Pigs' knuckles, hard-boiled eggs soaked in vinegar, pickles, and fish sandwiches were already on platters lining the bar, waiting for the rush.

"Come on in, son, and put the feed bag on. Course you gotta spend *some* money. Ole Bill Swan would go broke if you didn't."

"Hello, Bill," Slocum greeted the man. Of the people in New Orleans he had met so far, Swan was the most open with him. The former Live Oak Boy seemed to steer a course away from Rupert.

"I can tell from your expression that you're needin' some of my fine advice. Buy some liquor, grab a plate, and let's talk."

Slocum bought a warm beer and loaded a plate with food before joining Swan. The short delay gave him a chance to put his thoughts in order. He had been running around aimlessly all morning. It was time to focus his efforts and find Angelina.

"You're looking more prosperous," Swan observed. "Still carrying a bit of dirt, though." The saloon owner sniffed hard. "And burned. You got the smell of fire about you."

"What better place to come than the Fireproof Coffee House?" Slocum asked.

"What better place, indeed." Swan lowered his voice and stared hard at Slocum. "You surely have riled Clyde Rupert. The man's frothing at the mouth like a mad dog, wanting your hide. He's put out a five-hundred-dollar reward on your head."

"You interested in it?"

"I ran with the Live Oak Boys—and I regret it now. I wouldn't give Rupert the time of day. Hell, the bastard comes around with his men trying to extort money from me. Says the place isn't really fireproof. Hints he'll burn me to the ground. He knows what I'd do to him if he tried."

"You'd fight fire with fire?"

"I know where he lives," Swan said. Slocum was sure the man wasn't simply saying that Rupert lived somewhere. Swan meant Rupert had to come to earth sometime, and when he did, he'd find a world of trouble. "I don't go braggin' about being free of his extortion. Let the others do as they please. But he can't buy me, and I sure as hell don't pay off the son of a bitch."

"I'm glad you're still interested in the profit on a glass of beer," Slocum said, draining his.

"You're a cool one to have muddied the waters around here so much and still be in town."

"I got Angelina Delacroix out of the whorehouse where Rupert put her, but she doesn't want to go home. Says she's been shamed by all that's happened to her."

"Reckon she would be, coming from such an upstandin' Cajun family."

"Where would she hide?"

"How the hell should I know? I listen, but I don't know *everything* that goes on in New Orleans. Not even half."

"Where might she go? I haven't got a clue."

"Rupert is still hunting for her, so she's kept clear of the Live Oak Boys." Swan frowned. "Not too many places she might hole up. Can't go to any of her friends. They'd shun her." Swan shook his head. "You're on your own this time, son."

Slocum looked out the window and saw four of Rupert's men stalking by, their oak clubs resting on their shoulders like rifles. Nothing else about the men looked military. They were scroungy, beaten, and tattooed—and their eyes roved from side to side seeking Slocum.

Swan spun in his chair. "You got company, from the looks of those boys. Go on out the back way. If'n you tried the front, there'd be a powerful row. I can do without fresh blood on my floor. Just cleaned up from last night."

"Thanks," Slocum said, slipping toward the back way. He looked out into the alley. Two of the remnants from the revelry the night before moaned and stirred weakly. Slocum stepped over the two drunks and picked his way to the end of the alley.

A crunch of heavy feet against gravel warned him. He broke stride and ducked—in time. A heavy oak stave splintered against the wall where his head would have been if he'd kept walking.

Slocum spun around the corner, fists flying. He hit the Live Oak Boy a glancing blow on the ribs. The man staggered back, only to be replaced immediately by another. This thug swung his club with deadly precision. It landed hard on Slocum's upper left arm. Pain blasted through his shoulder and into his body, then the arm went numb. Try as he might, Slocum couldn't move it.

"You're gonna die, dude," yelled the man he had hit.

The one still swinging the oak bludgeon was too intent on bashing Slocum's brains out to talk.

Slocum reached to his cross-draw holster for his pistol. The oak stick batted his hand away. He turned away, then kicked like a mule, bracing himself against the wall. His boot connected squarely with the man's groin. His attacker let out a loud squeal like a stepped-on pig, then collapsed.

This didn't give Slocum much time to run for cover. He staggered forward, trying to get feeling back into his left arm. It refused every effort to entice it back to life. He crashed into the far wall of the alley, then bounced around. This time he had his Colt Navy drawn and ready.

The man charging him didn't seem to notice he faced a cocked and aimed six-shooter. Slocum fired.

For a heart-stopping instant, Slocum thought he had come up against another zombie. The Live Oak Boy kept coming, the rage on his face a contorted mask. But the man plunged past him and fell face-down in the dirt. He had died and never knew it.

The shot attracted unwanted attention. Slocum slipped back into the alley, then ran for all he was worth. It would take only a few minutes for the gang to swarm over the area. The killing of one of their own members would enrage them. Slocum wasn't sure if they'd start killing at random or engage in some more systematic search for him.

Whatever they did, he wanted to be miles away when they got around to hunting him down.

The problem of where to look for Angelina had changed. Slocum needed a safe place to hide, and he didn't know where that might be. Bill Swan was sympathetic but wasn't likely to provoke Clyde Rupert over the welfare of a drifter.

Not for the first time, Slocum considered going back to the *Cajun Queen* and stealing his bag before hightailing it west. The thirty dollars he needed came and went with frightening speed.

All thought of abandoning Angelina Delacroix to her

fate fled when he remembered the night of passion he'd spent with her. He cursed himself for a sentimental fool— and worse. But he felt honor-bound to return her to her family. He had known the chore wasn't going to be easy when he figured out the real problem. And he had come so close to getting her home.

His mind wandered down other paths. He had to retrieve Angelina, and he had to stay alive to do it. Where could he hide out?

The only answer that came to him was Marie Laveau. The voodoo queen offered some slim chance for sanctuary. She opposed Rupert. The friend of her enemy had to be an enemy, too. Slocum's footsteps turned quickly toward the Rue du Rempart and Marie Laveau's simple whitewashed house.

Twice he had to take cover and let patrols of angry Live Oak Boys pass. Even after he came out, he had the eerie feeling of being watched. Rupert sent only men after him. What would Doctor John send? More zombies?

Slocum tried to push aside such nonsense. The undead. Men who were brought back to life. Zombies. It couldn't happen. He knew it. His bullets had just gone astray in the dark. Flickering firelight often deceived the eye. He hadn't really shot Doctor John's disciple three times only to have him keep on attacking.

Without realizing it, Slocum's hand went to the lucky *gris-gris* Marie had given him after the attack on the bayou. He touched it and felt the chalky white powder oozing out. He jerked away from it as if it had burned his hand.

"Damned superstition," he grumbled. It was only superstition, he kept telling himself over and over as he made his way toward the woman's house.

Two small children played in the yard, chasing the chickens. An older girl, perhaps fourteen, sat on the porch. She seemed to know Slocum was watching. She raised her eyes from the needlework in her lap and stared straight at him. She was the spitting image of Marie Laveau. Slocum knew this had to be an older daughter.

The young girl motioned to Slocum. He glanced around, made sure the coast was clear, then vaulted the low fence and hurried to the porch. He sat on the stool he had used before.

"I'm looking for your mother." Slocum decided this wasn't a bad guess.

"She was expecting you," the girl said. "I'll go fetch her."

Marie Laveau came out from the house's cool interior after a few minutes. Of her pretty daughter, Slocum saw no trace. Even the smaller children in the yard had silently left.

"You are in trouble again," she said.

"The *gris-gris* you gave me isn't working," Slocum said.

"It works. Your problems are greater than its magic." Marie Laveau heaved a deep sigh. "You're still looking for Angelina Delacroix. It is written on your face for all to see."

"I found her," Slocum said. "And then I lost her." He quickly explained how Angelina thought she had been humiliated beyond bearing. "She can't go to her friends, and even if she did, I don't know them. I need help locating her."

"Why do you come to me?"

"Angelina is a key to unlocking the power in New Orleans," Slocum said. "She may only be a pawn to Rupert and Oram Delacroix, but she is useful."

"I care nothing about politics. Let them do as they will."

"Drive out all practitioners of voodoo? Drive out all your followers while supporting Doctor John? That's what you want?"

"You have heard how Monsieur Delacroix and his vigilance committee have struggled to wipe out all voodoo in the city?" Marie shook her head. "He cannot do it. The people need hope to survive. Their lives are poor and dreary. Voodoo gives them the chance to deal with their problems and even win."

Slocum said nothing. He'd taken a chance that Delacroix's position might be a total elimination of all voodoo practice. That explained why Doctor John and Rupert were such easy allies. And it went far toward forging a bond between himself and Marie Laveau. She might be able to fight off Doctor John's intrusion into her ceremonies, but she couldn't fight Rupert and Delacroix both.

"Only returning Angelina to her parents will break the hold Rupert has. Whoever does this might win Oram Delacroix's favor."

"I want nothing from that man!" raged Marie Laveau.

She subsided and rocked quietly in the chair, her eyes focused far down the street. Slocum knew she was working through all the possibilities. She had to decide to help him —and Angelina.

She stopped rocking and turned to Slocum. "Very well," she said. "I will help you. It will take some time to find where Angelina is hiding, but I will help."

Slocum didn't have to ask what the woman wanted in exchange. Oram Delacroix would have to stop his harassment of Marie Laveau's bayou voodoo ceremonies.

He could cross that bridge when he got to it.

14

Slocum paced nervously. He didn't like waiting and not knowing what was happening. Marie Laveau wouldn't turn him over to Rupert, that he knew. But he had no idea what other schemes might be cooking in her head. She had not gained her position of voodoo power by being stupid. Slocum worried that she might decide she could do better on her own—better without his aid than with it.

If she found Angelina Delacroix and didn't tell him, that would be all right. Slocum would hate to lose the balance of the hundred-dollar reward Constance Delacroix had promised, but at least the young woman would be returned to her home. But what else might Marie Laveau do besides return Angelina?

The voodoo queen might decide to use the young woman against Oram Delacroix much as Rupert and Doctor John were doing.

Slocum glanced over at two of Marie Laveau's children. They were five or six years old and played quietly behind the house. He had been playing nursemaid for them for over three hours. The sun was dipping low over the horizon, and the oppressive heat was lifting a mite. This did nothing to make Slocum any cooler under the collar.

He was a man of action. He had to be doing something instead of just waiting.

"You surely are as jumpy as a centipede with the chilblains," one of the children said. "You got to learn patience. That's what Mama all the time tells us."

Slocum knew patience. During the war he had been a sniper, and this had required infinite amounts of patience. He had to lie in wait for hours—once days—to get the right shot at the enemy officers. A Yank would ride up, his gold braid shimmering in the sunlight. When he was a perfect target and not a second before, Slocum would squeeze back on the trigger.

Soldiers didn't fight a battle nearly as well without officers as they did with.

Slocum knew patience—but not now. He was the hunted. Rupert's men sought him everywhere. And they were also looking for Angelina. He knew he ought to be out seeking the lovely young woman's hiding place rather than pacing in Marie Laveau's backyard. He knew it, yet he had decided to rely on the voodoo queen's sources of information.

He found himself in a real dilemma. He had chosen to trust Marie Laveau, but he couldn't really trust anyone.

"Mama does not cheat anyone," one of the children said. "She never has. It's not in her."

"What?"

"You was thinkin' Mama was going to double-cross you," the small boy said. "She won't. Trust her. Trust Marie Laveau."

He hadn't realized he was so transparent that even a six-year-old boy could fathom his thoughts.

Slocum laughed and started to reply when he caught a flash of bright red at the side of the house. Marie Laveau, her head bound with the brilliant silk *tignon*, came around the house and stopped just in front of him. She looked as if something pained her greatly.

"You didn't find her," Slocum guessed.

"No, I found her. I knew I could. There are only so many places where she could have gone."

The pieces clicked together in Slocum's head. He remembered the woman who had brought him to Constance Delacroix. "I should have thought of it myself. She went to Lottie for help."

"She did," Marie said. "But there's trouble. I wasn't the only one to know Angelina's mind."

"Rupert?"

"His men have surrounded the house where Angelina now hides. A friend of Lottie's has let Angelina use the house, but the Live Oak Boys lie in wait. They want bigger game than just Angelina."

"Who?" asked Slocum. "Do they think her father will come for her?"

"They wait for you, Mr. Slocum. They want you badly. You have stung Clyde Rupert's ego. You have disgraced him. His men snicker at him behind his back. Even the soiled doves of his brothels make jokes about him. He is not a man to accept this easily."

"What will he do if I don't spring his trap?"

"He will tire of waiting and fetch Angelina. You are a splinter in his side, but Angelina holds the key to power in New Orleans. He will not forsake that in exchange for revenge. Doctor John will not allow it."

"Their alliance is shaky?"

Marie Laveau shook her head. "They have an understanding. Doctor John is not one to permit others to fritter away his hard-won influence, though."

Slocum worked over how he could turn Rupert against Doctor John. Nothing came to mind. He had no hold on either of the men. He was well-nigh powerless, in fact. He had started out wanting only to get back the money stolen from Preston Chambers. The chore had turned into a major undertaking.

"You can still leave New Orleans, Mr. Slocum," the woman said. "This is not your fight."

"I won't leave her," he said. "I promised her mama to bring her back, and I will."

"You are a fool," Marie said, but her tone carried no sting.

He smiled crookedly and nodded. "Reckon so. Now where is it I can find Angelina?"

Slocum decided that he needed an army to get Angelina Delacroix from the house. The ramshackle building stood on poles to allow ventilation beneath the floorboards. This prevented him from sneaking in and reaching those inside without Rupert's men seeing him. Huge trees stood a distance away, but their limbs, heavy with colorful flowers, afforded no easy highway into the house.

His scouting of the house showed no fewer than eight Live Oak Boys waiting to nab him should he try to get Angelina out. The thugs weren't too bright, but he didn't think he could divert their attention long enough to get in and out with the young woman before they caught on. He had to do something more.

What? No answer came to him.

He needed to get a message to Angelina without any of those outside knowing. Deciding on the only course, he left the house and walked toward Canal Street and the Delacroix mansion. From what Marie Laveau had told him, he knew he would run into Lottie. The Delacroix's servant brought food to Angelina about this time of day.

"Mr. Slocum!" the woman called, seeing him before he spotted her. "What you doin' down heah?"

He grabbed her arm and pulled her under an oak tree, its dangling limbs forming a bower where they could talk without being seen from the street.

"They know Angelina's in the house," he said. "We've got to get her out."

"What you talkin' about?" demanded Lottie. "Angelina's not in any house I know of." He saw by the set of her shoulders that she was lying.

"There's no time to argue. Rupert and his gang will get tired of waiting for me to show up soon. When they do, they'll go after her. And this time what they do to her won't be half as nice as before."

"Half as nice! Why, Mr. Slocum, they—"

"I know what Rupert did to her," he said. "I just want to get her back to her family."

"She won't go. No, sir, she told me she won't. She been shamed something fierce." The woman's face hardened into resolve. "I can't go against her wishes in this."

"Rupert will use her, then kill her. Neither of us wants that. Will you help me get her away?"

"You sure about the Live Oak Boys being all round the house?" Lottie looked worried now. She nervously ran her hand across the handle of the wicker basket she carried.

"They've got it boxed in tighter than a drum," Slocum said.

"What do you want me to do?" Lottie finally asked.

Slocum told her.

The sun had sunk behind the misty horizon hours earlier. It had taken Slocum longer to steal the carriage with its single horse than he had thought. As it was, he worried that the horse would be strong enough for the task ahead. The animal looked in good shape, but he would put demands on it that it didn't normally need to respond to.

He patted the horse, then took a deep breath. It was time to get Angelina out of the house.

Slocum swung the carriage down the street in front of the house. He had examined the back alley and decided this was the smoother ride, therefore best for what he needed. When Lottie saw him coming, she dropped the burlap curtain over the front window. In the house the light from the single lamp grew brighter.

Slocum heard Rupert's men mumbling among themselves at the increasing glow within the house. When the flames licked at the roof and came out the windows, an uproar sounded. Ten men came out of hiding, all intent on the fire inside the shack.

No one moved until a black woman came running from the house, waving and gesturing. "Inside!" she cried. "A white girl's trapped inside. Save her, save her!"

She pulled her tattered scarf down around her face and stumbled into the arms of a burly thug. The man shoved her aside roughly and dashed for the house.

The woman had been left alone on the street when the Live Oak Boys rushed to the house to save Angelina Delacroix. This was what Slocum had been waiting for.

He snapped the reins hard and got the carriage moving along at a good clip. He barely slowed, but as he came abreast of the woman, he reached down and grabbed her outstretched arm. He swung her in front of him. She landed heavily on the seat beside him.

"Lottie," she gasped out. "Did she make it out?"

Slocum looked over his shoulder and saw Lottie staggering from the raging inferno. Sparks had set fire to her sparse clothing. The Live Oak Boys wanted nothing to do with another black woman, not when they thought Angelina Delacroix was still inside the inferno. Shouting curses, they kicked in the door and one was even brave enough to dive into the fire to find Angelina.

Slocum smiled crookedly. He hoped they all burned to death in the conflagration.

"How is she, Mr. Slocum? Please, I can't see!"

Slocum pushed the woman back into the seat. He didn't want any of Rupert's men, who weren't feeling particularly brave, seeing his passenger. He turned the corner and hazarded a quick look at the towering flames and choking smoke rising from the house.

The woman who had been on fire rushed out and fell into a puddle of water. Steam rose as the fiery clothing was extinguished. She shook herself like a wet dog and rose. Lottie waved to them that she was unhurt.

"She made it all right," Slocum told Angelina, who was rubbing at the soot on her face. Up close it was obvious she was no black woman. The soot had been put on clumsily and showed white patches through it. If they hadn't waited for nightfall, none of Rupert's men would have been fooled by the disguise.

Slocum kept the carriage barreling along. When he reached Canal Street, he turned up it. The carriage wheels rattled against the cobblestones. They raced past trolleys and other carriages. Slocum didn't want to stop until they were safe.

"No, Mr. Slocum, no! You can't take me home. My father will kill me as surely as Clyde Rupert."

"He's your father," protested Slocum. "He'll have to listen. None of what happened was your fault. They held you prisoner."

"He won't understand," she said glumly. "He can't. It's not in his nature."

"I'll make him understand," Slocum said. He applied the reins to the horse, but the animal began to flag. It was an older horse and not used to such exertion. He pulled back as foam began flecking the bay's flanks. If he killed the horse, it wouldn't do any of them any good.

"He won't. I know him," she said disconsolately.

"If I promise not to take you there, will you promise not to run off?"

"Yes," she said. This compounded Slocum's problem. He had rescued her from a trap. Where did he go now? The only places he knew were likely to be watched by Rupert's scoundrels.

Bill Swan's Fireproof Coffee House was an appealing spot, but Slocum knew better than to go to Gallatin Street with Angelina. Tongues would wag so hard it might cause a hurricane wind along the short street. And he couldn't put Swan on the spot like that. The man was friendly—but he wasn't a friend.

"Where are we going?" she asked.

"There's only one place I can think of. And I don't know how welcome we'll be."

Slocum turned the carriage into the French Quarter and down Rempart Street. If Marie Laveau wouldn't hide them for a few days, he didn't know who would.

15

"No. Go away. I have done all I can do for you. If Rupert finds out what I have done, he will kill me, kill my children." Marie Laveau stormed around the small room, waving her hands and motioning emphatically for Slocum and Angelina to leave.

Slocum stood his ground. "You're already involved. Look at the circle of salt around your house. Does that mean you don't already fear Doctor John's voodoo?"

"His *gris-gris* is not as strong as mine," the woman said haughtily.

"No, it isn't," Slocum said in a soft voice. He pulled out the bag of lucky powder she had given him. He balanced it on the tips of his fingers before letting it fall back against his chest. "Marie Laveau is the voodoo queen of New Orleans. There can be no other."

"There *is* no other," the woman said forcefully.

"Then why does Marie Laveau fear Doctor John and Clyde Rupert?"

Dark eyes bored into him, then she laughed. The sound

came rich and full and vibrant. "You are a clever man, John Slocum. What can they do to me and mine that they have not already tried? My charms protect my children."

"Your wits protect them," Slocum corrected.

"There is no difference between wit and voodoo, at times," the woman admitted. "But this is not solving your problem—or mine in how to deal with you. You cannot stay here. They will kill everyone in my family to get to you."

"Isn't there somewhere out of town where we could stay?" Slocum asked. "It won't be long. I want to convince Angelina to return to her family."

"That will take much doing," Marie Laveau said, eyeing the lovely young Cajun woman sitting in a corner of the room with her hands folded in her lap. "Her spirit has been harmed more than her body. Mending one is difficult. Mending the other . . ." She shook her head to show that it was an almost impossible task.

In that Slocum had to agree. He had seen healthy men just give up and keel over dead. Their will had been broken and they had just . . . died. There was no other explanation for what happened. On the other hand, he had seen men broken and beaten and shot up so bad there was hardly a drop of blood left inside, and they had fought all the way back to life.

Resolution meant as much as body. Maybe more.

"They will come here soon," Marie Laveau said, deep in thought. "We can decoy them for a short while, but Rupert is a cunning man."

"And Doctor John?"

She looked at Slocum as if he had spit on her. "He is nothing. Those who believe in voodoo will come to me. My *gris-gris* is stronger. He thinks only to harm. I seek to heal. Always the two forces oppose one another."

"Good triumphs over evil?" Slocum asked, amused.

"We shall see, Mr. Slocum." He followed her from the house to the backyard. Marie went to the horse tethered there and patted it. The poor animal had been pushed to the point of exhaustion. "The carriage will do you no good. Take the horse. I will give you a map to a small shack in the Bayou St. John."

"Where you hold your ceremonies?" he asked.

"I know the swamps better than anyone else. Doctor John cannot find you on *my* sacred ground."

Slocum remained silent. He didn't want to remind the woman that Doctor John and his men had broken up one ceremony on "her" ground. The voodoo king had succeeded in sneaking up on her unnoticed and would have killed everyone if fate hadn't dealt Marie Laveau a kinder hand. Slocum touched his six-shooter. He knew he'd be needing it again before he got Angelina home to her parents.

"I don't want to go into the bayou country," protested Angelina, hearing what Slocum and Marie Laveau were discussing. "That's no fit place for a lady of my breeding."

"It is if you want to stay alive," Slocum said. He swung the woman up and onto the horse's bare back. He mounted behind Angelina, his arms around her as he took the reins.

"Here is the map, Mr. Slocum," Marie Laveau said, quickly sketching in the dirt. He studied the map until he had it memorized. He nodded curtly. She erased the tracings with a quick movement of her foot. "Go with God."

Slocum didn't hear the rest of what the voodoo queen said. He guessed she was mumbling a protective spell to keep them safe from Rupert and Doctor John. His own brand of spell rested on his hip. Let the voodoo *papa-loi* send all the zombies in the world against him. He'd show them that a well-aimed bullet was the cure for living.

"This isn't going to work, John," Angelina said as they rode through the darkened streets to the north and west of the French Quarter. "They will find us. I know they will."

"We need the time to lay low and work out a plan," Slocum said. "You trust Marie Laveau, don't you?"

"Lottie does," the young woman said. "I'm not sure

how much of the voodoo I believe and how much I don't."

"I feel the same way," he admitted. "I've seen a few things that I can't explain, but I don't think I'm going to convert to cutting the heads off chickens just because of it."

Angelina shivered and wrapped her arms around herself, in spite of the warm breeze blowing off the bayou. "That's Rupert's favorite way of letting his enemies know he's serious about doing them in. I saw him do it to a customer at Mrs. Cunningham's who refused to pay up after spending an hour with another girl. Rupert slit his throat, then put the chicken claw into his mouth."

"I've seen it, too," Slocum said grimly. Preston Chambers' death still haunted him. He owed Rupert for that. On sudden impulse, he asked, "Did Rupert ever entertain any farmers in the brothel?"

"Farmers?"

"Their names are Ben and Josh."

Angelina shuddered again. "Them! They're pigs! Worse!"

"He does know them, then?"

"They're his cousins. I don't know where they're from, but it's not around here."

"Baton Rouge," Slocum said. So the two hayseeds were Rupert's relatives. Slocum smiled without mirth. He had thought something like this might be the case. That explained why the two disgruntled farmers had contacted the leader of the Live Oak Boys the instant the *Cajun Queen* docked.

"How do you know them?"

"They're just two more scores I have to settle," Slocum said, not wanting to go into it. They rode in silence for almost an hour. He tried to recognize the landmarks Marie Laveau had put on the crude map. The darkness masked much of the landscape, but he thought he had found the right path into the bayous.

Another half hour of fighting mosquitoes and jumping every time a bit of dangling moss stroked gently over his face brought them to a small shelter made of termite-eaten wood.

"Home, sweet home," Slocum said, dismounting. He helped Angelina down. She looked at the house with more than a little skepticism. He didn't blame her. This wasn't some fancy hotel in the Vieux Carré or the best stateroom on a fancy riverboat.

"Would . . . would you look inside first?" Angelina asked in a quavering voice. "I don't like surprises."

Slocum understood her uncertainty. He loosened the leather thong over the hammer of his Colt Navy and thrust the six-shooter ahead of him into the house. A burlap sack hung down for a door. Pushing the door hanging aside, he slipped into the house. The floor seemed solid enough, but cracks and wormholes large enough to fall through dotted the entire shack. A loud chittering sound caused him to spin, hand flashing to his weapon.

Demonic red eyes glared at him in hate. He drew his pistol but didn't fire. The rat, larger than many ship's cats he had seen, dived through a hole in the floor and vanished. He didn't doubt it would return—and with friends.

He poked at the small black pot in the center of the room. Someone had built a fire in it for cooking. The thought of food made Slocum's belly growl in protest. It had been too long since he'd had anything decent to eat.

"Come on in, Angelina," he said. "The place seems safe enough." He didn't mention the rat as the woman hesitantly peered inside. She summoned up more courage and came in.

"I tied the horse under the oak at the edge of the clearing. It's able to crop at some grass. It'll need water, though."

"So will we. This isn't fit to drink." Slocum sloshed around water in a pair of mason jars.

Angelina laughed. "You know what they say about water from the Mississippi River. It's too thin to cultivate and too thick to navigate, so there's nothing left to do but drink it."

"A good way to get cholera," he grumbled, putting the sealed jars back on the floor.

"There's a blanket that doesn't look too pest-ridden," Angelina said. She shook it out and a cloud of insects took wing. "I'll get some grass. We can use it for a mattress."

Slocum let her go about the pointless little domestic chores while he scouted the marshy area surrounding the shack. The ramshackle cabin stood at the edge of a clearing that was hardly noticeable from the path through Bayou St. John. A body'd have to be looking hard to find this isolated place, day or night. Slocum checked the horse and saw that Angelina had cared for the animal as well as she could. He let the horse drink a bit from a puddle that seemed less scummy than others. Then he returned to the cabin.

He paused for a moment before he pushed back inside. Slocum tried to collect his thoughts. He ought to let Angelina sleep. She had been through hell—and it wasn't anything compared to what they were likely to see in the next few days.

Slocum entered silently, and for a moment he thought Angelina Delacroix had hightailed it again. There was no sound at all in the shack. Then he saw a faint band of silver moonlight slanting through a hole in the roof and falling across naked skin.

"John," she said softly. "I want you. I *need* you!"

"You should sleep," he said, feeling like a damned fool. He knelt beside her. She lay nude on the blanket. The moonlight danced along the sleek lines of her hips and thighs, shadows hiding delectable portions of her anatomy.

Angelina turned slightly. The moon's quicksilver spilled across her breasts. The tiny coppery buttons on each succulent mound of breast was hard, firm, vibrantly erect. She reached up and took his wrist. She pulled his hand down to her chest. He felt the warmth of her breath as she kissed his hand. The heat of her body as she thrust her breasts into his palms. The liquid warmth of her center as she moved his hand into the forbidden territory between her argent thighs.

"I need you," she repeated.

"You're so beautiful," he said, hardly trusting himself to speak. His voice was on the verge of cracking with emotion. He found himself needing her, too.

Slocum hated to take his hand away from the dampness between the woman's legs, but he had to. He shucked off his gunbelt and then quickly followed that with his fancy jacket, shirt, and trousers. He kicked his boots aside and lay beside her, her naked flesh moistly pressing into his equally damp flesh.

Their mouths met, unsure at first, then with greater desire. Slocum stroked along the woman's firm chin, down her swanlike throat, and touched the lobes of her ears. She moaned softly and pressed even closer to him. Her long, coltish legs drifted apart and wrapped around his. He felt the wetness on the top of his thigh as the young woman began undulating up and down slowly.

"I need more from you, John. I need more!"

His tongue darted out and lightly teased her shell-like ears. He thrust his tongue deep into her ear and rolled it around. She arched her back and sobbed something he didn't understand. He wasn't going to stop to needlessly ask her to repeat it. He licked and sucked and nibbled down her throat, to her shoulders, down farther to the twin mountains of her quivering breasts.

He repeated the kissing and licking until the taut nipples throbbed with lust. He thought they might explode at any instant.

As he was orally attending to her body, Angelina was working on his. Her slender fingers stroked and her fingernails dug into his broad back, urging him on. As he worked ever lower on her supple body, she laced her fingers through his black hair and guided him in an erotic movement she found most arousing.

And all the while her hips moved relentlessly up and down. She clung to him like a snake climbing a tree. The wetness turned slicker on his leg. Slocum felt his length inflating until it pulsated painfully. He gasped when Angelina reached down and up the hot length of manflesh and began stroking.

"Not too much," he cautioned. "You're going to make me rush this—and I want it to take all night."

"Rush," she urged. "Rush now, then we can spend the night doing it slowly."

She tugged so insistently at him that Slocum rolled atop her and found an immediate berth where he had been fingering her. One instant, only the humid night surrounded him. The next, a sheath of clinging, velvety female flesh crushed down in all directions. It took his breath away. For a moment, he simply remained motionless, reveling in the sensations blasting into his balls.

His loins refused to let him remain still for too long. He pulled back, Angelina's fingers gripping fervently on his buttocks. She tugged him back into her, half sitting up to kiss him. Slocum bent over, his lips seeking hers. He started the ages-old rhythm of a man loving a woman, his hips working with deliberation.

Every inward thrust caused her to gasp and sob with new desire. She pleaded for him not to leave as he slickly slid from her. Snowy white thighs lifted and parted. Slocum felt as if he was being flattened by the woman's clutching innards.

He began stroking with more power. He made no effort to keep the pistoning of his hips smooth and even. Lust was taking its toll on his control. Sweat poured from his body, as much from the exertion as the naturally warm bayou night.

Each stroke lifted Angelina off the blanket. She rolled back, twisted around him, and gave his buried shaft an added thrill. Slocum sucked in his breath and tried to control himself, if only for a few more minutes.

He failed. The woman's beauty, the passion of her love-making, the need hidden in his loins all conspired to make him spill his seed. He felt the fiery tide rising inside and was unable to stop it. It spilled over into her yearning interior.

Angelina gasped and rocked as stark delight seized control of her senses. She shrieked out her lust, then relaxed as the edge went off her wanton desires. "That's what I needed, John," she said.

Slocum sank to the blanket beside her, exhausted. But he wasn't allowed to sleep. Angelina hadn't been joking about wanting to savor his hardness through the night. To his surprise, Slocum was able to rise to the occasion quickly enough. And this time the sensations lasted until dawn.

16

Angelina woke up screaming. Slocum jerked upright on the crude bed and put his arms around her, trying to calm her.

"John," she sobbed, burying her face in his shoulder. "I'm cursed. He . . . Doctor John has put a terrible spell on me. I'll never be whole again. He's robbed me of my soul!"

"Nonsense," Slocum snorted. "Voodoo has only as much power over you as you let it."

"I *feel* it. I . . . I don't know what he's done, but he's stripped me of my soul. I'm not human anymore." Angelina shoved away and got to her feet. She had a wild-eyed look that Slocum didn't like. She was working herself up into a conniption fit.

Slocum felt like a fool trying to argue with her without his pants on. He fumbled around and pulled them on and felt better for it. This made it seem that he had a measure of authority. He got his boots on and stood up.

"It's only a nightmare. Doctor John's back in New Orleans. No one knows we're out here." He swatted at a buzzing mosquito that disputed this claim.

"I saw him. He came into my dreams, and he was evil." She put her arms around herself and shuddered. He tired to comfort her again, but she wanted nothing to do with him. Slocum remembered the long, languid night after they'd dulled the razor edge of their lust. She hadn't seemed crazy then.

"We're safe out here. You heard Marie Laveau. She's got strong *gris-gris* and won't let anything happen to us. She knows how to protect us." Slocum took the bag of white powder from around his neck. He'd felt silly wearing it. He finally knew what it was good for. He handed it to Angelina. "Take this. Marie made it especially to ward off Doctor John's spells. It'll protect you."

"It's too late," she said, but she took the tiny bag. It hung around her neck and dangled between her voluptuous breasts. Slocum had to take a deep breath to keep down the earthy thoughts rising up in his head. He shook free of the notion about taking Angelina's mind off her nightmare. The night had well-nigh exhausted him.

Still . . .

Before Slocum could make the suggestion, he heard a rustling sound outside the shack. He paused for a moment, straining his every sense. It might be nothing more than a rank wind blowing across the treacherous swamp surrounding them.

He heard the sound again.

"Stay here," he said. He put his finger to his lips when Angelina started to question him. She looked frightened, but Slocum was sure this brief scouting trip of his wouldn't amount to a hill of beans. No one could know they were here. He belted his cross-draw holster on and checked his Colt. The ebony-handled pistol rested easy in his hand. He peered through a wide crack in the wall to see if he could surprise whoever or whatever had made the noise.

"Might be an alligator coming up out of the swamps," he said. "I'll be right back."

Slocum wasn't sure his six-shooter was the proper weapon for gator hunting, but it was all he had. If nothing else, he might be able to frighten one of the massive beasts. He doubted if he could do much harm with the pistol to an alligator, not with their thick skins.

The small clearing was empty. The first light of dawn had turned the sky gray and pink in anticipation of another scorching day. Slocum wiped sweat from his forehead and tried to remember the last time he'd had a bath. He stunk to high heaven, and there wasn't a part of his body that wasn't sticky with sweat and bug-bit.

Slocum put his back to the shack's rickety wall and made a slow circuit, quick green eyes trying to penetrate the shadows cast by the trees. A sucking noise echoed through the clearing—and it wasn't made by anything natural.

Slocum cocked his pistol and went hunting. He drifted like a ghost toward the nearest tree, then began working his way around the clearing, just out of sight. He heard nothing until he got near the spot where they tethered the horse.

Slippery, sliding sounds came to him. Slocum went to soothe the horse. The animal bucked and tried to tear free of its reins. Rather than grab the bridle and pull the rearing horse down, Slocum looked for the cause of its agitation.

At first he thought it was a log—but no log moved with such astonishing speed. Slocum got off three quick shots before he saw the ten-foot gator fully. All three of his bullets had bounced off the beast's flat head, and now the enormous reptile was pissed. A huge mouth filled with teeth opened and snapped shut with a stark ferocity that Slocum had seldom seen.

He jumped up and caught a sagging tree limb and pulled himself up to safety. The gator reared higher than Slocum thought possible and almost took off his right leg. Only a quick kick and a jerk to get himself over the rough tree limb saved him.

"Come on, friend," Slocum urged. "Rear up for me again. Just once more."

The alligator roared its anger—and Slocum fired point-blank into its mouth. This time the bullet had the desired effect. The alligator slithered away sinuously and vanished into the deep swamps from where it had come.

Slocum dropped to the ground and went after the gator. He wasn't the kind to wound an animal and let it go off somewhere to die. He'd finish the job, if he could.

He found the gator a dozen yards in the direction of a pond covered with green scum. He circled warily, not sure if the alligator had died or was merely lying there waiting for him. A frown creased his forehead as he neared the reptile.

A length of light chain was fastened around the alligator's neck. Slocum touched it with the toe of his foot. The alligator had been kept as a pet—and the chain hadn't been broken. There weren't any bright scratches on the links to show that it had used its prodigious neck muscles to pull free from its bonds.

"Angelina!"

Slocum knew he couldn't reload as he ran through the sucking, soft bayou land. He had two rounds left. They'd have to serve him well if his suspicions were true.

He stopped himself from dashing to the shack. If Angelina had been kidnapped, he didn't want to run into the teeth of a trap. The ten-foot alligator's deadly razor-toothed jaws were enough to last him for the rest of his life.

Staying in shadow, waiting for a bit more sunlight before making his approach, Slocum got around so that the sun was behind his back. The light might confuse anyone inside the shack waiting to ambush him. He walked as if he was stepping on eggshells as he crossed the open space between the trees and the shack.

Spinning, he put his back to the shack's wall. He

strained to hear. No sounds came from inside.

He twisted around and shoved his six-shooter into the doorway, ready to fire.

The run-down cabin was empty—except for a mocking reminder. In the center of the room was a decapitated chicken.

Slocum rode disconsolately back into New Orleans. Doctor John had kidnapped Angelina again. The voodoo priest had left the chicken to show his power, to prove that his *gris-gris* was stronger than Marie Laveau's. Slocum had considered trying to track Angelina and her captors through the impenetrable swamps but had given up on the notion after only a few minutes.

He could track with the best through the mountains, across prairies, or even across barren deserts. In the bayou he couldn't even keep a clear idea what direction he was headed in, much less follow another's spoor. The land didn't take a footprint for long. The smells assailing his nose assured his quarry of easy escape. Upwind or downwind had no meaning when everything smelled of rot and decay. And he couldn't see for more than a few feet through the thick undergrowth.

He considered returning to Marie Laveau and telling her what had happened but reconsidered. He trusted the woman, but not too much. She was, after all, mixed up in voodoo. In Slocum's mind that made her suspect. He doubted she had told Doctor John where Slocum and Angelina had gone to hide out, but he couldn't be sure.

Clyde Rupert had ways of making even a statue talk. Someone with Doctor John's voodoo power might be able to do more. Slocum had seen how Marie Laveau doted on her children. A threat to them might be all it took for the woman to reveal Angelina's hiding place.

Slocum touched the hollow of his throat where Marie's lucky *gris-gris* bag had ridden for so many days. His lip curled into a sneer. It hadn't done him much good, and it sure as hell hadn't given Angelina the protection the voodoo queen had claimed.

He couldn't go to Marie Laveau. He had to choose another course. He saw only one. Slocum rode into town from the northwest, found Craps Street and followed it until he got to Canal Street. From there he rode into the rich section of New Orleans.

He almost changed his mind when he reined back in front of the Delacroix mansion. What did he expect from Oram Delacroix when the man had denied his daughter had even been kidnapped? Politics meant more to him than blood.

Slocum dismounted. He wasn't going to let Angelina stay in Doctor John's hands. The voodoo priest had muttered about using her as a sacrifice in his pagan rituals. No one deserved that, especially Angelina Delacroix.

He thought about going around to the servant's entrance, then decided against it. He wasn't dressed for proper receiving, but he didn't give a damn. He had to talk to Oram Delacroix.

"Mr. Slocum!" came the frightened cry from one side of the large veranda running the entire length of the house's front. "Don't you go in there!"

"Lottie, I've come to see Mr. Delacroix. Is he at home?"

"Oh, he's gonna be powerful mad if you go bargin' in on him. He got friends in the drawing room. Powerful friends."

"Then they can help him get his daughter back."

"What happened?" the maid asked, her eyes big and round. "Doctor John didn't grab her, did he?"

Slocum's grim expression gave the woman all the answer she needed. Lottie crossed herself and began muttering some sort of protective spell. Slocum had run out of patience with voodoo.

"I'm going to see him," he said flatly.

"Please, Mr. Slocum. Come around back," Lottie

pleaded. "I'll go fetch Mrs. Delacroix. She'll want to talk to you 'fore you go botherin' Mr. Delacroix."

Slocum went around to the back, against his better judgment. It wasn't right for a father to abandon his daughter the way Oram Delacroix was.

"Just sit yourself down and I'll find her. Please." Lottie was begging. Slocum did as she bid, fuming as he waited. Ten minutes later, Constance Delacroix came from the rear of the house, looking distraught. She used a small feather fan to keep the air moving across her flushed face, and she looked as if she'd rather be meeting with the devil than John Slocum.

"Mrs. Delacroix, Doctor John has your daughter again. I got her back," he said, almost stumbling over the words. Slocum decided against telling the woman about Angelina's imprisonment and forced service in Rupert's brothel. "But before we could return here, she was taken prisoner once more."

"No," Constance Delacroix said in a small voice. "I was afraid of this."

"All this has something to do with your husband's activities, doesn't it?"

"He's trying to clean up the dock area. He wants the police to put pressure on the Live Oak Boys. He has found the officers who are being paid off and is threatening them."

"And Clyde Rupert isn't taking it lying down," Slocum finished. "There's more to it, though. Your husband is on a crusade to stamp out voodoo in New Orleans."

"He's trying to do so much for New Orleans. And his enemies are so strong."

"Have you even told him Angelina has been kidnapped?" Slocum wasn't sure what went on in this Cajun family. Their ideas of honor and propriety might be different from his. He couldn't believe Angelina would rather die than return to her father and admit that Rupert had forced her to work as a whore. It hadn't been any of her doing.

"He . . . knows," she said. "It is difficult speaking with Oram about such things."

"I'll do it,' Slocum said. "He has to know. Let him use his contacts with the police to put pressure on Doctor John."

"No!"

"Why not?" asked Slocum.

Both women looked frightened.

"Bad *gris-gris*," muttered Lottie. "Doctor John has put a curse on the house and everyone in it. Even the lucky *gris-gris* wreath on the door can't protect us."

"Bullshit," Slocum exclaimed. "He works best through fear. He can't do a damned thing to you unless you let him."

An agonized scream cut through the still morning. Slocum spun, hand going to his six-shooter. Across the veranda stood another black servant. The man's eyes had gone wide, and white showed all around. He took a step forward, then toppled like a felled tree.

Slocum raced to the man and rolled him over. The man's tongue lolled out, and his eyes, sightless in death, stared upward. They were already glazing over with a foggy coating.

"What happened to him?" Slocum asked.

"He was cursed," Lottie said in a tiny voice. "Doctor John cursed him."

Slocum examined the man for some clue as to the cause of his death. He found nothing. The man had simply . . . died.

17

"He just upped and died," Lottie moaned. "It's been like that forever and ever round heah!"

"Be quiet, Lottie," ordered Mrs. Delacroix. She took her servant's sudden, unnerving death better than Slocum would have thought. The delicate feather fan fluttered, and color tinged her cheeks, but she was bearing up well after watching a man simply keel over and die on her back porch.

"You mean this has happened before?" asked Slocum, perplexed. He stood and stared at the body. He saw no reason for the man to have died. He just had.

"Twice before," Constance Delacroix said in a weak voice. "Doctor John is warning Oram not to continue his campaign against voodoo—and the Live Oak Boys."

"Might be poison," Slocum guessed, staring at the corpse. He had no knowledge of how voodoo priests worked their seeming magic. All he knew for a fact was that it wasn't witchcraft. There wasn't a supernatural explanation for this death. The servant had died from *some-*

143

thing tangible, something real, something anyone could use if they knew the carefully guarded secret.

"I should tell Oram," Mrs. Delacroix said. "He is going to be upset."

"Tell him about his daughter, too, while you're at it," Slocum said bitterly. He was reaching the end of his rope with these people. "Is that going to upset him unduly, finding that the same man who's been killing your servants has kidnapped Angelina, also?"

"Sir, you do not understand my husband."

"Reckon you just said a mouthful, Mrs. Delacroix. You know what the rumors are about Angelina, don't you?"

"Lottie has told me. Doctor John intends to use my daughter as some pagan sacrifice in his evil voodoo ceremonies."

Slocum told her about the chicken with its head cut off. "Doctor John left that as a warning for me. But I don't scare that easily, Mrs. Delacroix."

"Perhaps it is best that you forget this entire matter, Mr. Slocum. Here, let me pay you the balance of what's owed. You have done more than I expected."

"I don't want your damned money," Slocum snapped. "I said I'd get Angelina back, and I will. Come hell or high water, I will!"

If Angelina couldn't return to her parents for reasons of twisted honor, Slocum felt equally bound by his own code of honor to rescue her. She had been free. If he hadn't insisted on getting her back to her family, she might not be in Doctor John's hands now. They could have simply ridden west.

Slocum paused as he considered the thought racing through his mind. Would Angelina even want to stay with him? She was a woman of good breeding, used to expensive clothing and only the best life had to offer. He looked around the neatly kept grounds of the Delacroix mansion. He could never offer her anything like this. Hell, he was hard-pressed to come up with the thirty dollars to fetch his bag off Captain Stephan's riverboat.

"Thank you, Mr. Slocum. I don't know how I was ever lucky enough to find an honorable man such as yourself for this sorry task." The color rushed to her cheeks and she averted her eyes, as if she had made a bad mistake in judgment and was trying to make amends.

"I'm doing this as much for myself as for Angelina," Slocum admitted. And he was. Preston Chambers' death had to be avenged. And he wasn't the kind to take kindly to having all his money stolen. Slocum wanted it back— and a share of revenge on Clyde Rupert, his worthless cousins, *and* Doctor John.

He had a heap of catching up to do. He set about doing it.

Mounting the tired, protesting horse, Slocum turned once more toward Rue du Rempart. Marie Laveau was his only hope.

"It's all falling apart around me, Mr. Slocum," the voodoo queen said in an aggrieved voice. "I try to do my best, to cast my finest spells, but they aren't working right."

"So Doctor John's really stronger than you?" Slocum said, feeding her anger.

"There are tides of power you know nothing about," she snapped. "Doctor John is riding the crest of a tidal wave now. Evil is triumphant over good, but only for the time. The tide will wash out and leave the faithful high and dry."

"Fine words," scoffed Slocum. "What does this do to help get Angelina back?"

"Nothing," said Marie Laveau. She sat on the front porch of her small house, elbows on her knees and chin cupped in her hands. She stared into the misty distance. The sun was setting, and the pressure of time wore heavily on Slocum.

"Where's he likely to perform his ritual? If I can—"

"I have not been able to find out, Mr. Slocum. And

believe me, I have tried. Doctor John is most secretive."

"There must be someone who can tell you. Or someone who'll tell me." Slocum cracked his knuckles, unconsciously wishing he had Doctor John's scrawny neck under his fingers.

"No one will speak of it. They fear him."

"How did he kill the Delacroix's servants?" Slocum asked suddenly.

"Fear," she said. "He cast a parting spell, and they frightened themselves to death."

Slocum started to tell her what he thought about it, then remembered the cases where faith had saved men. There was no reason intense belief in evil couldn't also kill.

"How do I find where his ceremony is to be held?" Slocum looked up and saw a full moon rising in the velvet-black sky. Only the night before he and Angelina had made love under its light. Now she was going to die unless he found her.

"I do not know," Marie Laveau said. "Fear is the key. No one will speak to me out of terror for what he might do to them."

"He's got followers. I killed one of them," Slocum said, thinking out loud. "I can find one and follow him to the ceremony."

"It will not be easy. You cannot blend into the crowd. You stand out like a cue ball on a billiards table." She laughed at his obvious discomfort at the comparison.

Slocum took his leave of the woman, not knowing how he was going to find his way to Doctor John's deadly voodoo ritual, but knowing that he had to.

Slocum would have let out a whoop of glee if he hadn't been hidden so close to the man. His quarry looked around nervously, touching the tall silk stovepipe hat repeatedly, as if it burned his head. Slocum had come to the area in the French Quarter just north of Barracks Street on the off chance he might see another of Doctor John's emissaries.

He had.

Slocum had slipped into the doorway of a quiet Spanish-style house and waited. The man, dressed entirely in black and uneasily wearing the distinctive hat, paced back and forth on the corner. Slocum was almost as nervous as the man. He had considered taking him prisoner and forcing him at gunpoint to tell where Doctor John was, but he had discarded this idea when he realized the man's fear of the voodoo priest might be greater than his fear of death.

Better to watch and wait a spell longer, no matter how it chewed away at his guts.

Slocum's patience paid off. A dozen men and women drifted down the street like ghosts. They joined the man in the stovepipe hat. He spoke briefly with each. Money changed hands. Only when another five joined the group and the rite was repeated did the black man motion for the others to follow. No one spoke. All moved as if they were going to their own funeral.

Slocum trailed them at a distance of a block. Something told him to fall back even more when they reached the edge of the Vieux Carré. And he was glad that he did.

Others joined the procession. If he had been any closer, he would have been spotted. More than three dozen pilgrims huddled together, speaking only in whispers when they talked at all. Even at this distance, Slocum felt the tension in the group. They were going to witness more than the usual voodoo ceremony tonight. They were going to see a human sacrifice.

Wagons came, and the people piled in. Slocum wished he had his stolen horse, but to have brought the poor animal would have given him away immediately. Slocum looked around for another means of transportation. He smiled slowly when he saw a carriage driver jump out and duck into a nearby house.

Slocum didn't know what assignation awaited the man inside, but when he came out, he had lost his horse. This had worked before for Slocum, and it worked now. He rode bareback until he turned a corner and was out of sight of the house.

He reined back and the horse protested. It wasn't used to a rider; pulling a carriage was work enough.

"There, there, it won't be long," Slocum soothed, patting the horse on the neck until it quieted. He didn't want the balky horse giving him away. Too much depended on silence.

Slocum caught up with the procession just outside New Orleans. He fell back and let them go their way. He wasn't sure if they had posted guards along the route. If he had been Doctor John, there would have been lookouts every mile or two ready for trouble.

It was this caution that saved Slocum. Through the darkness of the swamp they were entering, he saw the guide wearing the tall hat stand up and tip his hat, then sit back down quickly. Slocum reined back and got off the road. He didn't know what the signal meant, but he couldn't pass muster.

The thought flashed through his mind that he might have been spotted earlier and this was the signal to eliminate him. He dismounted and hunkered down beside the road, hidden by the trunk of a large banyan tree. When no one came to challenge him, Slocum left his horse tethered and made his way farther into the bayou.

When he reached the point where the signal had been given, Slocum looked around. High in a tree sat a man with a rifle. Scouting around showed no other guards.

Slocum knew he could get by the guard, but did he want to leave a man with a rifle at his back? He'd need to make a quick escape when he found Angelina. Other considerations sent Slocum back to his horse to make a wide circle around the guard.

He could never reach the man without alerting others. A single shot might not be enough to bring the man down, and Doctor John's anxious disciples would hear the gunfire. Climbing the tree without being heard was out of the question.

Keeping far enough off the road to avoid being seen, Slocum found himself sloughing through swamp. The horse began protesting such abuse and forced Slocum back toward the road. He hoped that no other sentries had been posted.

Slocum found the trail again by studying the road. The heavy wagons had cut deep ruts into the marshy ground. He followed the tracks through three forks in the road. He dismounted once more when he heard chanting and saw sparks rising above the trees. He left the horse and advanced on foot.

When he came to the edge of the clearing, he knew he had been successful. He had found Doctor John's voodoo ceremony.

A huge bonfire blazed in the center of the clearing. Around it danced a ragged line of Doctor John's disciples, sinuously twisting to a steady hypnotic drumbeat. Slocum circled, keeping just behind the line of trees. He wanted to get closer to the throne set up at the far side of the area.

His trigger finger itched with need. He wanted to find Doctor John and send a bullet through his putrid heart. But the voodoo priest was nowhere to be seen. The throne stood empty, its highly polished wood gleaming in reflected firelight.

And of Angelina Delacroix he saw not a trace.

Slocum settled down for a long wait.

An hour of dancing had exhausted the revelers. It had taken its toll on Slocum, too. He kept drifting off to sleep. When the drums suddenly stopped, he came awake with a start, hand going to his holstered pistol. He had a harder time seeing what was happening; the fire had died down to embers and had not be rekindled.

The worshipers in the clearing dropped to their knees and began a low chant. From the side came Doctor John, flanked by four huge black men stripped to their waists.

From the way they walked, Slocum suspected something was wrong with them.

"Behold!" cried Doctor John. "Behold my power!" He drew a knife that gleamed in the moonlight, now giving an eerie illumination to the scene. The voodoo priest raised it, then drove the sharp blade directly into the chest of the man closest to him.

Slocum gasped. The sound that might have given him away was drowned out by shrieks and cries of fear and amazement from the tight knot of worshipers. The blade entered the man's chest, then came out bloody—and the man had only staggered slightly. He still stood passively in front of Doctor John.

A zombie! Slocum knew it would be harder stopping Doctor John now that he had four bodyguards of the undead.

He shook himself and tried to push such nonsense from his mind. These four weren't dead men brought back to unholy life. They might be drugged. Doctor John might be performing like in a raree-show. It might all be sleight-of-hand. Slocum didn't know how the trick was done, but it had to be a trick.

There wasn't any such thing as a zombie. At least he hoped there wasn't, because he would never be able to rescue Angelina if there was.

The crowd gasped again when Doctor John sent two of his zombie assistants to fetch the young woman. They dragged her from the shadows. Her sudden appearance made Slocum's heart almost stop. Never had she looked so beautiful. In the moonlight, her flesh took on a breathtaking glow. She was dressed in a white, flowing gown that bannered behind her as she was pulled into the clearing.

"She will die this night so that we may *live*!" cried Doctor John. He motioned to his helpers. They dragged Angelina toward the throne and forced her to kneel.

Doctor John ascended the throne and seated himself, staring down at his victim. "You will not show fear. You will rejoice in your death this night. Through your blood, we will *live*!"

Angelina said something that caused the man holding her right arm to jerk. She gasped as he drove her forward, her head banging into the bottom of Doctor John's throne.

Slocum rose and moved closer to the throne. All eyes were on the spectacle there. No one would see him—until he struck.

"You will rejoice with us. You will not fear your death. You will welcome it, as you welcome my kiss."

The men lifted Angelina and carried her to Doctor John. The voodoo priest grabbed the girl's head and kissed her full on the lips. She jerked back, horrified. Then her struggles died and she hung limply in the men's grip.

"To the altar. Prepare her for the sacrifice."

The drums started a slow rhythmic throbbing that sounded like a heart beating. Slocum saw them carrying a now limp Angelina to the sacrificial altar. He didn't know what Doctor John had done to her, but all the fight had fled her young body. She lay peacefully on the slab of rock beside his throne.

The drums picked up tempo and the crowd rose from their knees. They began dancing slowly. As the beat increased, their dancing became wilder, less inhibited. Doctor John began chanting. He harangued them into a blood fury. His voodoo disciples shrieked and cried and tore their own clothes. And still he waited.

Slocum moved closer to the altar. Angelina's eyes were open. She stared at Doctor John but did not move when he reached over and ripped open the diaphanous dress she wore. Her breasts were bared to the moon above.

"She dies that we may live!"

Doctor John raised the knife to drive it into Angelina's heart. Slocum cocked and aimed in one smooth movement. The slug hit Doctor John in the forehead. The voodoo priest staggered and turned. Slocum's second round hit him in the center of the back. Doctor John fell forward, dead before he hit the ground.

The drums never slowed their beat. The dancers paid no attention to their priest's death; they were too caught up in the ritual.

Slocum darted out and grabbed Angelina's hand, pulling her off the rocky altar. "Come on, run!" he urged. She just stared at him. He saw by her dilated pupils that she had been drugged.

He slapped her hard. A red welt formed on her white cheek. The pain of a second slap began to bring her around.

"John?"

"Run!" He turned and saw that the four guards serving Doctor John had noticed that their priest was dead. It took them several seconds to understand what had happened. When they did, all four turned and began lumbering in Slocum's direction.

The heavy drumbeat covered the sound of his Colt Navy firing four more times. But even though all four slugs found their target, none of the men went down—or even noticed the passage of hot lead through their bodies.

"They're drugged, John. They can't feel any pain. I don't know how he did it, but there's nothing you can do to them when they're in this state."

"Run," he told Angelina, pushing her into the swamps.

Slocum saw how poorly the four men walked. He dashed after Angelina, then spun, grabbed a fallen limb and waited for the zombies. When the first of them ducked low to avoid an overhanging limb, Slocum swung as hard as he could. He connected with the man's kneecap. The sick crunching noise told of broken bones. The man toppled over, unable to stand on his damaged leg. But not once did he utter a sound. He stared up at Slocum with baleful, dead eyes.

"Where are we going, John?" asked Angelina, as she struggled through the bayou.

"Keep going. We've still got three of them on our trail."

Slocum kept moving through the bayou, cutting left and right as the whim struck him. After a half hour, he knew they had outdistanced the trio still after them.

And he also knew he was hopelessly turned around in the swamp. He had no idea how to get out.

18

"We're lost," Slocum admitted to the frightened woman. "I cut away from the path and doubled back so many times I lost track of direction." He stared into the murky depths of the bayou. In the distance growled a deep-throated bull alligator. Swarms of vicious, bloodsucking insects buzzed around their heads. But he hadn't heard the sound of another human since they plunged into the rank swamp to get away from Doctor John's bodyguards.

"But we can't be. Just go back to the clearing . . ." Angelina let out a tiny cry when she said that. "No, not that. We can't go back *there*."

"I understand, and we're not." Slocum wished he could return to the site of the ceremony, though. From the clearing he could find his horse and the road leading back to New Orleans. Under the dense overhang in the bayou, he couldn't even see the full moon. All that filtered down to the ground was a weak light that did more to confuse him than to help him find their way out.

"John!" shrieked Angelina. She grabbed his arm.

He had his pistol out and aimed the instant he saw the cause of her alarm. An alligator easily fifteen feet long opened its mouth not two paces distant. It let out a loud, nerve-shattering roar that shook Slocum.

"Back away," he said. "We can't fight it." Even as he spoke, he knew how futile it would be to try firing—his six-shooter was empty. He hadn't had time to reload. Even if he had, a cannon would have given them a better chance against the reptilian monster.

They edged away, and the gator went back to a logy sleep. On drier land, Angelina threw her arms around Slocum and cried bitterly. "I'm sorry, John. I'm trying to be strong, but I can't. Doctor John cursed me. He took my soul."

"What happened before he put you on the altar?"

She clung to him even harder. "I don't know. I had told myself I was going to die fighting him. Then he kissed me. I felt a sharp sting on my lip as if I'd eaten something acid. Then . . . I don't know. I felt as if I were drifting on a cloud."

"He must have transferred a drug to you in the kiss," Slocum said. "That's the only explanation for your behavior. It might be the same one he used on those four men."

"I . . . I'm a zombie now?"

"No," he said sharply. "They might have been given huge doses of whatever drug he used. But he only wanted to numb you, not rob you of all sensation." Slocum didn't add that Doctor John had been doing her a great favor. She would have died under his flashing knife and never known it.

He led her in a direction away from the alligator. He had no idea where they were going. After an hour, he finally decided the best they could do was rest. The morning would give them a better chance of escaping the interminable bog stretching all around them.

"Here," he said. "Can you climb the tree? It'll be safer there."

"No, John, it won't. Snakes. Big snakes of all kinds sleep there during the night."

It took Slocum a second to realize it hadn't been Angelina answering him. He pivoted, Colt cocked and ready for action. The barrel centered on Marie Laveau.

"Where'd you come from?" he demanded.

"I know the bayou country well. It took much doing, but after you had gone I learned where Doctor John was to hold his ceremony. I came to do what I could."

"You would have challenged his power?" Slocum asked. He motioned in Angelina's direction.

"I would have. The power is on me now. I can counter anything of his." The woman pulled herself up to her full height. Slocum had never seen a queen, but Marie Laveau looked the part. She had a dignity and at the same time an arrogance that could convince even the worst skeptic.

"You can cure me? You can bring back my soul?" cried Angelina.

"Your soul is not lost, child," the voodoo queen said softly. "Doctor John only imprisoned it. I know how to release it. It will not be easy, but I can do it if we work together. I am *mama-loi*. I am the voodoo queen of New Orleans. No one knows the chants and unlocking spells better."

This was what Slocum wanted to hear. Angelina had to be given hope before she would admit to being whole again. There was one other question he had to ask.

Marie Laveau answered before he could put it into words. "This way Mr. Slocum. We are not far from the road and my carriage." She laughed heartily. "You would have blundered about for days in this boundless swamp without finding your way."

"How far are we from the clearing where the ceremony was held?" he asked. Before Marie Laveau could answer, he stopped her. "Never mind. I don't want to know."

They walked less than a hundred yards before passing through the deserted clearing. Doctor John's body was gone, as was all trace that any illicit voodoo rite had been held here.

Marie Laveau finished the last of her charms. She turned to Angelina and handed her a blue candle with seven notches cut in it. The young woman took it hesitantly.

"Go on, take it," urged the voodoo queen. She thrust it forcefully into Angelina's trembling hand. "You will light the candle. Do you see the cuts in the side? Good. When the candle burns to the first notch, write your name on a piece of paper and set it on fire."

"From the candle flame?" asked Angelina.

"No. Use this." Marie Laveau poured brandy into a saucer. "Light this and set the paper ablaze from its cleansing fire. Blow out the flame. Then drink the brandy. Repeat this every time the candle burns past a notch."

"And then?"

"Then we will bury an apple with the ashes of the seven slips of paper placed inside it. When the apple withers and dies, you will be reborn and your soul will be released from its bondage."

"How long will this take?" asked Slocum.

"The burning will occupy seven hours," said Marie Laveau. "The burying of the apple, its withering and rebirth will take longer. Perhaps a week. It is a short enough time for freeing her soul from the evil chains Doctor John placed on it."

Slocum didn't believe a word of this voodoo nonsense, but he saw that Angelina hung on Marie's every word.

"If this will keep you occupied for a while, I've got other business to tend to."

"Rupert?"

Slocum nodded. He had ended Doctor John's foul life. He intended to do the same with Clyde Rupert, his two hayseed cousins, and any of the Live Oak Boys who got in his way.

"Be blessed in your task, John Slocum," the woman

said. She turned back to Angelina and handed her a lucifer.

As Slocum slipped out the door of Marie Laveau's house, Angelina Delacroix lit the notched blue candle and began the recovery of her soul.

Slocum walked toward Gallatin Street. For all the time he thought he had spent thrashing about in the bayou, it was hardly three in the morning. The saloons were doing their usual roaring business. Drunks staggered down the streets and whores propositioned them. From the darker alleys came the sounds of men receiving brutal beatings as they were robbed. All in all, a normal night in the French Quarter.

He decided the best place to stop for the information he needed was Bill Swan's Fireproof Coffee House.

"Well, well, well, there's a face I never thought to see again. Buy yourself a drink, friend, and come sit with me," said the saloon's owner. The huge man slapped Slocum on the back hard and pointed toward a table at the far side of the room. Gambling on a new rat-killing dog was in full swing, and others drifted into the back room, where a dance hall band played badly.

Slocum got his beer, noting how little money he had left. Still, for all the trouble he'd been through in the past few days, he couldn't count it all as lost. He had gotten Angelina back—again.

"What you been up to?" asked Bill Swan. The bulky man took a deep drink from the bottle of red wheat whiskey in his hand. He wiped his lips and vented a sigh of infinite relief at the whiskey's effect on his protruding belly.

"I killed Doctor John tonight," Slocum said straightforwardly. The warm beer slid down his throat. He wasn't sure he'd ever tasted anything better in his life.

"You did? No loss to New Orleans," said Swan. "That's not where I'd've thought you'd be on a night like this, though."

"Where should I have been?"

"You missed all the fun. Oram Delacroix finally got the balls to take on Rupert. He upped and formed a vigilance committee. About two dozen of the damned fools barged in on Rupert and twice that number of his Live Oak Boys down on Girod Street."

"What happened?" Slocum wasn't sure he wanted to find out. Swan's cheerful tone said the outcome was about the same as putting a fierce dog against a rat.

"Rupert's men tore 'em apart. Blood and guts everywhere. Wish I'd known Delacroix was going to do a damn-fool thing like that. Could have taken bets and made a bloody fortune."

"Is Delacroix dead?" Slocum didn't want to have to tell his daughter her father had died on the very night she was being sacrificed in a voodoo ceremony.

"Don't think so. A few of his vigilantes hightailed it when the going got too rough. A couple of them that Rupert caught were beaten to death outright, just for fun. I think he's saving Delacroix to make an example of." Swan cocked his head to one side and stared at Slocum. "You *really* kill Doctor John?"

"I did."

"Son of a bitch. That's going to make Rupert madder'n a wet hen. He thought he had the city locked up tight. With Delacroix his prisoner, he could have called all the shots in New Orleans. Doctor John's death is going to make it harder for him to keep control."

"Marie Laveau is again ruler in voodoo matters," Slocum said.

"Rupert and Marie never got along. Sparks are gonna fly over this, mark my words."

"Where is Delacroix being held?"

Swan's hearty laugh drowned out even the brass band playing loudly and off-key in the back room. "You're not the type to call it a night, are you? For most men, killing Doctor John would be the work of a lifetime. He was one tough hombre."

"Rupert killed a friend of mine and stole our money. I want the money back—with interest."

"You mentioned that before. He's got his two sodbuster cousins with him, too. I understand they did real good in helping him stop Delacroix's vigilantes."

"You're agitating, Swan."

Bill Swan grinned even more broadly. "Damned right I am. Should I take bets on this?"

"If I had any money, I'd bet on it."

"How much you got on you, Slocum?"

Slocum fumbled in his pockets and came out with a little less than four dollars. The thought crossed his mind that he still needed thirty dollars to get his bag off the *Cajun Queen*, but this seemed like an impossibility now.

"I'll lay you odds of a hundred to one," said Swan. "Four hundred dollars for your four, all on the outcome of you against Clyde Rupert tonight."

"Make it two hundred to one and I'll get rid of his two cousins," said Slocum.

"Hell and damnation but you drive a hard bargain. Two hundred to one it is, but you got to leave the money with me."

Slocum shoved it across the table. Either he'd be back to collect eight hundred dollars from Swan, or he wouldn't be needing anything. He was sure New Orleans had the equivalent of a potter's field, even if it meant being taken out to the bayou and getting fed to an alligator.

He finished his beer and went hunting for Clyde Rupert.

19

Slocum went to the dock area at the end of Julia Street to start his search for Clyde Rupert. Bill Swan hadn't been specific about where the man might have taken Oram Delacroix, but the saloon owner had said it had to be in this general area. This was the stronghold for the Live Oak Boys.

The strong smell of the Mississippi River assailed Slocum's nostrils and made them flare. For all the mud and filth floating there, it looked like heaven to him after spending most of the night floundering around in the swampy bayou country. He wished he had time to take a proper bath, but he had business to attend to.

That business was Rupert.

He paused briefly and looked at the *Cajun Queen* sitting pretty at dockside. Its sides had been repainted, making it look like a new boat. Its decks were laden with cargo to take north. The riverboat would be sailing in a day or two at most. Slocum considered taking the money offered by

Mrs. Delacroix and simply leaving this madness behind. There was only death ahead.

The cold rage inside him began to heat when he thought of all that Rupert had done—he and his two no-account cousins. Money was part of it, but revenge burned brighter in him than ever. He couldn't let Preston Chambers' death go unanswered.

Slocum smiled wickedly. In addition to Chambers' money and that promised by Mrs. Delacroix, Slocum wanted to collect on the bet he'd made with Bill Swan. With a little luck he could leave New Orleans with a thousand dollars burning in his pocket—and the sense of revenge achieved.

He stalked the wharves, hunting for any of the Live Oak Boys. If he could find one, he could beat the information he needed out of him. But Slocum drew a blank. The docks were more deserted than any of the fancy cemeteries scattered around New Orleans. He might have fallen into the center of the Sonoran Desert for all the people he found lurking around the usually bustling docks.

"We busted 'em up good," came a faint voice. Laughter followed. "Gimme the bottle. Don't hog it, damn you!"

Slocum recognized the voices. He moved toward a warehouse a block away from the wharf. A door opened into the large warehouse and let a thin slice of yellow light sneak away. He worked his way closer and peered inside.

Ben and Josh sat facing each other, a bottle of cheap whiskey on an overturned crate between them. They had already finished one bottle and had drunk half of this one. Josh bent forward and held his belly. Slocum felt some satisfaction that the wound he had inflicted on the treacherous farmer was still bothering him.

"Howdy, gents," Slocum said, lifting his Colt Navy and pointing it a point midway between the two farmers. "You're just the folks I've been meaning to find."

They swung around, too drunk to be frightened. Ben

said, "Well, if it ain't the cardsharp off the riverboat. Come and have a drink."

"In hell!" snapped Slocum. "Where's Delacroix?"

"Who? Oh, you mean that vigilante fellow our cousin's got hog-tied." Josh frowned. He wasn't as drunk as his brother and finally realized he shouldn't be telling Slocum anything. His hand touched the spot on his belly where Slocum's slug had buried itself in his flesh.

The alcoholic fog dimming his brain lifted, but not far enough or fast enough. Josh knew he was in trouble but thought he could do something about it. The farmer tried to draw the old Colt Dragoon stuck in his belt.

Slocum never hesitated. He sent a bullet ripping through Josh's brain. The man tumbled backward over a crate and lay sprawled, his pistol still stuck in his belt.

"You went and shot him again!" complained Ben. He stared at the feebly kicking corpse of his brother for several seconds. The enormity of the shooting finally penetrated his alcohol-besotted mind. "You *killed* him this time!"

He tried to pull his own gun, but Slocum took two quick steps and slammed the barrel of his six-shooter alongside the man's head. Ben sank to his knees, clutching at the spurting wound Slocum had opened.

"You're buzzard bait if you don't tell me where Rupert is."

"Why should I tell you squat?"

"You and that worthless brother of yours might not have killed Chambers, but you told Rupert to do it for you. That's good enough for me to splatter your guts all over this warehouse. I killed him. Do you think I won't cut you down where you stand?"

Ben looked up into Slocum's cold green eyes. A flare of courage took him. He started to spit at Slocum. The Colt Navy swung again and opened a new cut on the other side of his head.

"I don't want to get the sights out of alignment whacking you on the head. The next time I put a bullet through your putrid face. Where's Delacroix being held?"

"You won't kill me if I tell you?"

Slocum hated a coward. "Tell me," was all he answered.

"Cousin Clyde's got his prisoners in a building a block down the street. Me and Josh, we were standing guard and stopping anyone coming to disturb him."

"Yeah, sure," Slocum said. It was all anyone could have expected from the two farmers. They weren't even much good at shooting a man in the back. They'd chosen to get drunk instead of keeping a lookout as they'd been told. He cocked the pistol and put it to the side of Ben's head. "Listen good. If you don't get the hell out of New Orleans, the next sound you're going to hear is this."

Slocum pulled the trigger—after moving the pistol muzzle a fraction of an inch to the side. The wadding and powder set fire to Ben's hair. Slocum let the man put out the tiny blaze. Then he cocked the pistol again.

By this time Ben was racing for the door. Slocum let him go. He'd sooner shoot a snake in the grass than waste ammunition on the likes of the craven farmer.

Slocum took time to reload, then set off in search of Clyde Rupert. He didn't think Ben had lied—and he hadn't. A large building in the next block showed light through a dozen different windows. An unpainted sign over the door proclaimed this to be the offices of a company called Oak Staff Enterprises. Slocum knew it had to be Rupert's headquarters.

He scouted the building and found that it occupied an entire city block. It must have more ways in and out than a prairie dog town. That suited Slocum for getting in. He just didn't want Rupert using one of the myriad ways to escape justice.

Slocum carefully worked his way up a protesting drainpipe at the corner of the brick building until he got to a narrow ledge on the second floor. He swung onto the ledge and balanced precariously. A bit of old mortar broke off under his foot and went tumbling into the silent street below. He didn't think there would be any problem, since he hadn't seen any guards posted.

He was wrong. Three Live Oak Boys came from inside the building, more curious than alert to danger. Slocum clung by his fingertips to the rough brick front and tried to move his boots to get a more secure footing.

". . . heard something, I tell you." One thug swung his oak club back and forth, creating a swooshing noise that Slocum heard from a full story above the three men.

"Might be more of those damned vigilantes," said the second man. "You look that way. Me and Pete'll go this way."

"Better not split up," said the first one. "We almost had more'n we could handle before."

"I ain't had that much fun in weeks," spoke up the third. "I wanna bash in some more skulls."

"Listen to 'im," said the first.

"You're forgetting why we came out here. Shut up and let's check the place out."

Slocum fought to keep his footing until the trio below had stalked off in search of a ground-level invader. When they vanished around the corner, he moved to his right and found the window ledge. Gripping it, he recovered his balance and succeeded in pushing open the window. The creaking noise sounded louder to him than it actually was. In a flash he was inside the building and safe from view from the street.

He drew his six-shooter and walked gingerly through the fallen plaster and debris strewn on the floor. He poked open a door leading to walkway looking out over a large storage area. The place was darker than the moonlit streets. It took several seconds for Slocum's eyes to adjust to the difference in lighting. When they did, Slocum saw a half-dozen men gathered in the far corner of the room. He moved around the walkway until he could peer down on them.

He picked out Clyde Rupert immediately. The man stood to one side, drinking straight from a whiskey bottle. The other men in his gang had been drinking heavily also. Some staggered, and not a few had already passed out.

Slocum saw there was every reason for them to celebrate. Oram Delacroix slumped in a heavy wooden chair, his hands and feet bound to the chair's legs.

"Wake him up. I don't care how you do it. I want the bastard awake so I can gloat."

"But Clyde," complained one of the more sober Live Oak Boys on the floor, "we tried everything. You conked him good on the head. He ain't been awake since the fight."

"Get him awake. I want to tell him what I did to his little girl. I want to see the bastard's face when I tell him *everything*."

Slocum moved quickly and positioned himself above the men. Eight were still alert enough to give him problems; he had only six rounds in his pistol. He wished he had a double-barreled shotgun. He could take most of them out with two blasts, then finish the survivors with his six-shooter.

But he had only his trusty Colt. And Slocum knew exactly where he had to start the slaughter.

The man ordered to awaken Delacroix came back with a bucket of water. He heaved and sent it splashing over the man. Delacroix sputtered and stirred. Rupert hurried to him and grabbed a handful of hair and pulled until Delacroix stared upward.

From his vantage point Slocum saw that the man was still more unconscious than aware of his surroundings.

"Delacroix!" shouted Rupert in a drunken rage. "You thought you could stop me. You thought you were better than me. Well, you're not. I've got you by the balls, you worthless piece of shit!"

"What—" muttered Delacroix.

"I've really got you, and I've had your daughter. Do

you hear me?" Rupert shook the man. Slocum saw awareness returning to Oram Delacroix. "Do you know what I did to your daughter?"

"Angelina?" croaked out Delacroix. "What about her?"

"I'll tell you what I did. I—"

He was cut off by Slocum's cold voice calling down, "Good-bye, Rupert, you son of a bitch!"

The leader of the Live Oak Boys looked up in time to see Slocum's finger squeeze down on the trigger. The Colt's sharp report echoed throughout the warehouse.

Clyde Rupert died without uttering another sound. Then all hell broke loose.

20

Slocum dived for cover when the fusillade of bullets ripped into the wood walkway all around him. He knew he had killed Clyde Rupert. That filled him with a glow of revenge achieved, but he had to escape from this death trap to brag about it.

It took him several seconds to realize there was far more gunfire than he could account for. Bullets still winged past him, some missing by scant inches, but most of the shots came from below. Slocum wormed his way to the edge of the walkway and peered over cautiously. Rupert lay flat on his back. Slocum had drilled him square in the center of the forehead. Oram Delacroix was still bound to the chair, struggling to get free.

The Live Oak Boys had all taken cover. Slocum saw several of them reloading their six-shooters. They had already expended a cylinder's worth of ammunition. But at what? They weren't directing their fire at him now.

Slocum took a chance and gunned down a brutish man who seemed to be assuming Rupert's mantle of power. The thug slid down a rough wood crate, clutching his shoulder. Slocum hadn't gotten in a killing shot but had put the man out of action for some time. The amount of blood on the floor was silent testament to that.

"This way, men!" came a loud cry. "Show them no mercy! Kill the ruffians!"

Slocum slid back and watched as a wave of men carrying rifles and shotguns poured into the warehouse. They were momentarily held at bay by a hail of bullets from the Live Oak Boys. Then they surged again, their anger carrying them through the deadly rain of lead.

"Kill them. No need to let them live to stand trial!"

Slocum knew that the paltry vigilante group Delacroix had led before had grown in defeat. The few survivors must have rallied dozens of their fellow citizens. Behind the vigilantes came uniformed police. Few of them carried pistols, but all had truncheons they used with alacrity on any Live Oak Boy they saw. More than one young thug was given in kind what he had meted out for so many years.

"Stay back or we'll kill Delacroix!" called a trapped gang member. "We got him here." He grabbed the leg of Delacroix's chair and pulled him bodily to one side of the small space in the crates. For a moment he vanished from Slocum's view.

"You'll hang, by God," declared a police officer. "We'll let the lot of you swing if you harm him."

"He goes free—if we do."

The policeman held the vigilantes in check for the moment. Slocum knew their anger at the Live Oak Boys would boil over and they would come pouring through the stacks of crates at any moment. They didn't care if Oram Delacroix died. They wanted revenge for the injustices forced upon them for so long.

Slocum saw that all attention was focused on the two men shouting at each other. Oram Delacroix was pushed back, a pawn still waiting to be played in the deadly game. Swinging over the edge of the walkway, Slocum dropped to the top of a hardwood crate, then jumped to the floor of the warehouse. In a crouch, he went to check Clyde Rupert. The man was very dead.

Slocum reached inside the man's coat pocket and pulled out the distinctively hand-tooled leather wallet that had been taken off Preston Chambers' dead body. He flipped it open. It held less than three hundred dollars. Slocum let out a disgusted snort. He had hoped for more. He reckoned his half of their take from St. Louis would have been well nigh a thousand dollars.

But this would do. He stuffed the wallet into his jacket pocket and duck-walked in the direction of Delacroix's chair.

"Keep your damn fool head down," came the order from his right. "You don't want them blowin' it off, do you?"

Slocum shot the man giving the warning in the chest.

He hurried to kneel beside Oram Delacroix. The captive had regained full consciousness and glared at Slocum as if he was the devil incarnate.

"You'll hang for what you're doing," promised the bound man.

"Probably. It surely does go against my better judgment," Slocum said. He reached behind him and found the thick-bladed knife sheathed at the small of his back. He whipped it out and cut Delacroix's bounds with a single slash.

"What?"

"Shut up and follow me."

"Who are you, sir? What is the meaning of this?"

"The meaning is simple enough, even for a man like you," Slocum said. He didn't much care for Oram Delacroix or his treatment of his daughter. "I'll get you out of here in one piece."

"This will not save your miserable neck from the hangman's noose!"

"I'm not with them," snapped Slocum. "Your wife hired

me to . . . look after your daughter." Slocum couldn't bring himself to tell the man what he had done, or what had happened to Angelina.

"Angelina? I don't understand."

Slocum grabbed Delacroix by the collar and pulled him flat to the floor. His Colt Navy spat two shots and drove back a Live Oak Boy rising up ahead. Slocum saw that this path was cut off for them, and it would never do to try to surrender to the vigilantes. They'd shoot anything that moved as long as the killing fever was on them.

"This way. We can talk about it later." Slocum wiggled on his belly and moved deeper into the warehouse. He didn't bother to see if Oram Delacroix followed. When he jerked around and sat up to reload his pistol, he saw that the Cajun gentleman had stayed close behind the entire way.

"What of Angelina?" demanded Delacroix.

"Later. She's safe. Nothing's happened to her."

"Why should it have?"

"You don't know what was happening in your own house?" asked Slocum. "You don't know that your servants are keeling over dead?"

"No," the man said, puzzled by the question. "I've been involved in bringing these ruffians to the justice they deserve. Someone has already killed their leader."

"Rupert got what he deserved. He killed a friend of mine and robbed me," Slocum said.

"You shot him?"

"It was him or you," Slocum said. "He was going to cut your throat." The lie rode easily on his tongue. It made Delacroix beholden to him and kept the man quiet for a few more minutes.

Six-shooter reloaded, Slocum edged forward once more. He reached the wall of the warehouse without further encounter. Going along it, the gunfire far behind him now, Slocum found a barred door. He slid the iron locking shaft back and kicked open the door. Two Live Oak Boys stood outside, clubs ready.

Slocum cut them down.

"They deserved worse fates," Delacroix muttered. "They should have been hanged in public."

"There's still one of Rupert's cousins on the loose for you to hang," Slocum said. "His name's Ben. He looks like a sodbuster, but don't let that fool you. He's a mean-spirited killer."

They stood outside the Live Oak Boys' headquarters. Inside, the volleys came so fast and furious it sounded like a Gatling gun firing. Then the gunfire died down. Slocum guessed that the last of the gang had been dispatched.

"Sir, how may I thank you?"

"Don't bother. Your wife's paying me. I'll go fetch your daughter right away."

"I'll double your fee, sir. It is the least I can do."

"We'll talk about it after Angelina's back where she belongs."

"Wait. I'll go with you."

Slocum didn't give the man the chance to accompany him. He rushed off, turned the corner, and got the hell away from the site of the Live Oak Boys' massacre. Rupert and his gang had gotten what they deserved, but Slocum wasn't sure if Oram Delacroix didn't deserve the same fate.

21

Slocum neared Marie Laveau's house. He slowed and finally stopped, just staring at the simple whitewashed frame home. It was two hours past dawn, the sky already on fire with a new day. He had been through a lifetime of fighting this night, and he wasn't sure what the real outcome had been.

Doctor John and Clyde Rupert were dead by his hand, both dying within hours of each other. One of Rupert's cousins had been killed, and the other was being hunted down like a dog by Delacroix's vigilance committee. The Live Oak Boys' power had been broken for all time. No one could come in and pick up the pieces of power left behind by Rupert's death.

And Angelina Delacroix waited inside the voodoo queen's house.

Slocum wondered if it was worth his effort to see if Angelina had regained her soul through Marie Laveau's voodoo charms and incantations. Bill Swan had paid him the eight hundred dollar bet with alacrity, taking great glee in knowing his old enemy had perished. Slocum had little to hold him in New Orleans now, and he might be better off simply heading to the dock, forking over thirty dollars, and getting his bag back from Captain Stephan. He could even catch a ride up the river, to Baton Rouge or Greenville, Mississippi, or even farther. He had nothing to hold him in New Orleans.

Nothing.

He started to turn and go, but memories of the pleasant nights with Angelina drew him back as if he were on a string. He went up the steps and stood on the porch. He knocked lightly on the door. From within he heard a soft, "Come in."

Angelina sat at the far side of the room, melted wax on a low table beside her. She had burned down the blue candle to a nubbin. He wondered if she felt whole again.

"Don't go away, John. Please. Come in." She motioned for him to sit beside her.

"Where's Marie?" He didn't see the undisputed voodoo priestess of all New Orleans anywhere in the house.

"She had to go. Her followers demanded an immediate purification ceremony. A celebration. She's out at Bayou St. John right now."

"How are you?" he asked. Never had Angelina looked lovelier. There was color in her cheeks, and she seemed composed, at ease with herself and the world.

"It worked," she said simply. "As I sat and watched the candle burn down inch by inch, I felt my soul coming back." Angelina hiccuped. "The brandy helped, too."

Slocum had to smile. "I saw your father tonight." The young woman tensed and turned away. "He broke the back of the Live Oak Boys. They won't be a problem anymore."

He took her hand. She seemed limp now, the spark of vitality gone once more after his mentioning her father.

"You can go home. He doesn't know what happened to you. Unless you tell him, there's no way he can know."

"Rupert . . ."

"He's dead. I made sure of that. He never said a word to your father about what he did to you."

"Can I live the lie? *I* know what Rupert and Doctor John did to me."

"Can you live without your family? They don't know—and won't. You can go back. Your father's eager to see you." Slocum bit his lip at the lie. Or half lie, he mentally corrected. Oram Delacroix wouldn't be displeased to see Angelina again. The man hardly knew anything had happened other than his organizing of the vigilance committee.

"Now? I can go back right now?" she asked. Life again flowed in her.

"Yes," Slocum said.

Angelina leaned over and kissed him. The kiss deepened. He tried to push her away. This wouldn't do if she was returning to her life in prim and proper Cajun society. Angelina would have none of his hesitation. She gripped him with a surprising passion.

"Not yet, John. I don't want to go back yet. Just once more. One more time with you."

Her weight carried him to the floor. They lay there, arms around one another, their mouths locked together in a fervent kiss, tongues dancing back and forth, bodies striving against each other.

Slocum was never quite sure how it happened, but Angelina worked off his coat, gunbelt, and shirt. He turned to the simple dress she wore, one no doubt borrowed from Marie Laveau to replace the white sacrificial gown put on her by Doctor John.

The buttons opened easily. The twin mounds of her sumptuous breasts spilled forth. He took the right one in his mouth and applied suction. Angelina gasped with pleasure. His tongue danced over the hardening coppery nipple until he felt the young woman's pulse through it. Then he shifted to the other one, giving it the same attention.

Angelina squirmed and wiggled and kicked free of her dress while Slocum kissed and licked her breasts and belly.

His tongue dipped into the shallow depression of her navel before raking across the cornsilk-fine hairs on her slightly domed, heaving stomach.

His hands moved lower and positioned on each of her firm thighs. Her legs opened for him.

"I'm still a bit overdressed," he said. But he wasn't, not for long. Angelina shucked his pants off and exposed his long, thick shaft of needy flesh. She gripped it fiercely, almost painfully.

"I want you, John. I want you now. This will be the last time for me for a long, long time." She grinned almost shyly. "And it might never be this good again."

Angelina's grip tightened until Slocum gasped out. She pulled him directly toward her moist center. The purpled tip of his manhood touched the delicate nether lips, then sank in.

For both of them, time stood still. Slocum basked in the carnal heat boiling from inside the woman. She surrounded him like a perfect glove, gripping and twitching, stroking and caressing. When she began bucking up and down, lifting her hips and grinding slowly, he thought he would lose control.

His hands slipped under her. He caught up twin handfuls of assflesh. He tried to knead her buttocks into a new and even more wondrous form, but he failed. He couldn't improve on nature.

"Do it fast. I need you burning me up inside. Don't tease, John. Do it hard!"

He gripped her buttocks even harder and pulled her softly yielding body into his. Their crotches ground together in a mix of desire and love. He sank even farther into her and held it for only a moment. What Angelina wanted was also driving him.

He pulled out, paused as he rotated her fleshly ass, then slid forcefully back into her soft berth. She gasped. Her fingers began raking his back as her desires mounted.

Hips levering back and forth, Slocum started to build

speed. He kissed and licked but the real action was in his loins. His balls tightened into a hard sphere. He felt the lust boiling inside him, barely contained.

And Angelina!

She gasped and moaned and shrieked out in need. He filled her and more. Together they climbed a high peak, dallied for a moment, and then slipped down the far side. Arms tightly around each other, they lay exhausted. Slocum didn't dare speak. He didn't want the magic of the moment to slip away.

But it did. Angelina stirred and sat up, looking down at him. Her eyes were misted over with tears as she said, "I've got to go home. There's no other way, John."

He knew. Silently he turned and began dressing. He didn't look at her until he had finished. She sat there, ready to leave. Angelina didn't say a word when he held out his hand to help her to her feet.

Slocum hailed a carriage at St. Anne Street which took them to Canal and north into the area of lavish mansions and uncountable wealth. For a few minutes he wondered what it would be like having so much money. He couldn't imagine. To him the thousand dollars riding in his pocket was big money, but what was a thousand dollars to a man like Oram Delacroix? A few minutes' income? Less? Slocum had no idea.

The carriage stopped. He paid the fare and helped Angelina down. She looked elegant, in spite of the plain dress. She might have been a princess going to an extravagant ball in her honor.

He smiled. All trace of the ravishment she had endured was gone from her face. Inside might be another story, but outwardly she was again a member of this high society. He wasn't sure if the change came from Marie Laveau's voodoo—or his own magic.

"Angelina!" cried Constance Delacroix from the front veranda. The woman rushed out and caught up her daughter, hugging her tight. Slocum saw Oram Delacroix still on the veranda, a frown on his face.

Slocum left mother and daughter and went to the house. He tipped his hat in Delacroix's direction.

"I brought her back. She's been through a great deal, sir. I hope you can understand if she's a tad reluctant to speak of it."

"Then you can tell me, sir," Delacroix said coldly. "Exactly what *has* she been up to? My wife had not told me she was missing."

"Missing? Not that," said Slocum, lying. "The trouble with Rupert and his men sorely frightened her. She sought your maid's help."

"Lottie?"

"She trusts her, and rightfully so," Slocum said. "And Lottie trusts Marie Laveau."

Oram Delacroix stiffened. "What does she have to do with this?"

"She kept your daughter safe, even while your servants were being killed by Rupert and Doctor John."

"Voodoo," scoffed Delacroix.

"I share your opinion, sir," said Slocum. "However, Marie Laveau *did* protect Miss Angelina from harm. And she did successfully fight Doctor John, just as you did Clyde Rupert. The pair of you lifted the yoke that's been on this city for some time," Slocum said. He didn't bother telling his part in both men's deaths. Oram Delacroix wasn't the kind to take kindly to anyone sharing his limelight.

"She did, eh?"

"She's a powerful ally, sir," said Slocum. "She's taken quite a fancy to your daughter. And Miss Angelina admires her, too."

"Angelina never had a lick of sense," Delacroix said.

"Marie Laveau can be a *very* influential ally to someone like you with political ambitions," Slocum added.

"She did take good care of Angelina," Delacroix mused.

"Perhaps I should speak with this self-styled voodoo priestess."

"Couldn't hurt." Slocum took a deep breath. It was time for him to leave. He turned and stopped in front of Constance Delacroix.

The woman handed him a small white envelope. He started to refuse it, but she said, "Please, Mr. Slocum. I insist. For what you've done for my family."

"Thank you, ma'am." He looked at Angelina, but she averted her eyes. "Good day," he said, striding off.

He never looked back at the Delacroix mansion. This wasn't his kind of life, and there was nothing here to hold him long. With any luck, he could make it to the docks and ransom his bag from the captain of the *Cajun Queen*.

And then? John Slocum wasn't sure, but he was not staying in New Orleans. It held too many ghosts sure to haunt him.

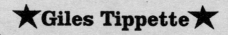